CUNNING Treatment

A NOVEL

JERROD R. DANIELS

Pentland Press, Inc.
England • USA • Scotland

This is a work of fiction. Names, places, incidents and characters either are used fictitiously or are products of the author's imagination. Any resemblance to actual events or places or persons, living or dead, is entirely coincidental.

PUBLISHED BY PENTLAND PRESS, INC.
5122 Bur Oak Circle, Raleigh, North Carolina 27612
United States of America
919-782-0281

ISBN 1-57197-212-9
Library of Congress Catalog Card Number 99-80017

Copyright © 2000 Jerrod R. Daniels
All rights reserved, which includes the right to reproduce this book or portions thereof in any form whatsoever except as provided by the U.S. Copyright Law.

Printed in the United States of America

To my daughter, Ki, my life-time achievement . . . to Desda Garner and Edith McCrory who taught me to love words . . . to Dr. Richard Marius who defined presence in a classroom.

Justice requires not subtle sophistries; It in itself hath fitness. But injustice being rotten at the heart needs cunning treatment.

—*Euripides*

CHAPTER 1

When the helicopter transporting Kip Fowler arrived at the hospital, the pace in the East Wing changed abruptly. The junior United States senator from North Carolina was severely injured in the crash of his small plane and required immediate surgery. Hurriedly, two of Raleigh's top surgeons made a final review of the stats on the young politician who had not regained consciousness.

"Hell, Chuck. What do you make of this? Do you know something about him I don't?" Dr. Horace Simmons was addressing his frequent surgery partner, Dr. Charles Cochran, who would again assist him in the operating room. He was referring to the blood analysis report that had just been handed to him by a nurse who quickly left the room, leaving the two men to finish their preparations. "The guy needs blood, and his own father isn't a match. Couldn't even be his father," the surgeon muttered, not wanting to make such a declaration too loudly.

"Well, make damn sure the staff doesn't get sloppy and talk to the press about this," Simmons added. "Or anyone else for that matter."

The two doctors were in a small office in the new surgical wing of Raleigh Memorial Hospital. They were cautiously preparing for a critical operation on the politically up-and-coming young senator from their state. Seated behind his cluttered desk, Dr. Simmons leaned forward, placing both his arms on the desk. Curious, he waited for his colleague's response to his startling observation.

Only minutes earlier, Kip Fowler had been rushed from the crash site of his twin engine Cessna at a small, rural airport in the mountains of western North Carolina. He was bleeding internally due to what was initially suspected to be a punctured lung. When his father, former senator Jonathan Fowler, arrived at the hospital, he volunteered to give blood for his only son's use during the operation. The elder Fowler was at that moment lying in a private hospital room and already in the process of giving a pint of his plasma for the person many viewed as a strong player in the approaching presidential race. Routine blood typing procedures were performed, but the results showed the patrician senior Fowler's blood to be incompatible with his son's.

"What about the senator's mother?" Dr. Cochran asked. He preferred to evade the question about the senator's father.

"I asked about her. She's off the coast of Alaska on a cruise and isn't scheduled to be back for another week," Simmons replied. "Her son's office is sending the message about the accident to her on the ship. Kip's wife is on the way here. But we've got to proceed whether it's with a family member's plasma or not. I ordered tests on several pints for AIDS and hepatitis. The senator's chief of staff called and personally made sure that was definitely ordered."

As soon as the governor's office had been notified about the crash, a special state plane had been dispatched to Washington to bring Senator Fowler's wife back to Raleigh. Gracie Fowler, along with the senator's chief aide and his secretary, would arrive within an hour. Members of the senator's Raleigh office staff were already at the hospital meeting with the press in a special waiting room in the East Wing.

Both doctors stood for a moment looking at the senator's medical records, each hoping in silence that the awkward fact before them would somehow go away. Each had known the elder Fowler socially in Raleigh for many years and had followed the rise of "Young Kip," as he was affectionately referred to in the Tar Heel State, from the ashes of his father's own career in the late '60s.

The year had been 1968. The newspaper headline summed up the situation in three bold words: "LIBERAL FOWLER

DEFEATED." As one of the few doves from south of the Mason-Dixon line, Senator Jonathan Fowler had paid the price for his outspoken opposition to the war in Vietnam, as well as for his unpopular stands on domestic issues. Dangerously oblivious to his more conservative constituency back home, Fowler championed liberal causes that he felt were crucial to the nation as a whole. However, his votes for reelection came only from his home state, and North Carolina voters said "enough" to Jonathan Fowler and retired him to his farm south of the state capital.

On election night, November 5, 1966, the suddenly soft-spoken, yet still defiant Jonathan Fowler read a hastily prepared concession speech to a large crowd of tearful followers gathered in the ballroom of the Sheraton Hotel. "I know each of you share with me tonight the sad reality of a defeat. Each of you has been there with me and my family all along the way. And it never was easy. We did what we did because it was the right thing to do. And I don't mean right wing." His attempt at humor brought only isolated pockets of muted laughter. "But I would like to think this country is a better place for what we did. I took it upon myself to say what I felt had to be said. I will never regret that. Not a single word. Never. My only regret is that I will not be there to see the causes we bravely embraced brought to their logical and just conclusions. I thank each of you. You have been loyal friends. And dedicated believers." He paused to catch his breath, then continued. "Most of all, I am grateful to my beloved Lenore." Standing beside her husband, Lenore Fowler managed a slight smile and nodded to the audience acknowledging the warm applause, only to again raise her head back to a proud position. She appeared even more defiant than her husband.

"Lenore has been my strongest supporter all these many years. And often she has been my inspiration. For if someone so lovely and gracious liked what I stood for, then I couldn't be all that bad." With two raised hands, he silenced the applause, determined to finish his message. "Yes, I have been guilty of looking beyond the borders of our beloved state. I truly believe a United States senator must address the bigger picture." He again paused and shook his head, as if to control his emotions. "Apparently, many thought I was mistaken to do so. But I will not apologize. I did what I did for each of you and for so many more who are not here tonight, some who may not have even ever heard of me. But most of all, I did it for all of North Carolina. Mark my words, when the definitive history is finally written on our tumultuous times, I will be proven correct. Thank you all."

With that declaration, Jonathan Fowler took his wife by one hand and their teenage daughter by the other and departed the political world forever. Only his son, Kip, was missing that evening in the proud man's parade away from the podium and away from the limelight he adored.

Listening to her father's remarks, the senator's daughter, Anne, a slender, honey blonde, stood beside her parents, as on so many occasions before. She smiled bravely and waved to favorite friends in the ballroom crowd. However, her younger brother was not to be seen on that momentous night. That had been the case on most occasions in his life. The senator's son had never been a feature in his father's campaigns. When asked, Lenore always explained that Kip was away at boarding school in New England. There were few, if any, pictures in newspapers to even remind the people of North Carolina that their senior senator had a son who was growing up in Washington, D.C. Some suspected that was just another indication of the Fowlers' tendency to be away, mentally as well as physically, from their home state, or perhaps it was something else altogether. Something no one had ever put their finger on.

However, by the mid 1980s the roles had been drastically reversed. Jonathan Sr. had withdrawn dramatically from the political scene after his defeat. On the other hand, his son quietly moved back to North Carolina after attending Yale and graduating from Georgetown University's School of Law. Kip Fowler methodically proceeded to mend his family's political fences, all the while paying his dues to insiders in the state's Democratic Party. He wisely adopted a more acceptable, moderate political philosophy and was elected the state's youngest governor after only one term in the state Senate in the late 1970s. Eventually, as the hard working junior United States senator from North Carolina, the wavy-haired, handsome Kip Fowler became a favorite of eastern and mid-western Democrats. He was frequently mentioned as a very plausible balance to any number of senior party leaders who might head the national ticket in the next presidential election. After years of conservative Republican control of the White House, political commentators sensed the appeal that a ticket which included Kip Fowler and his moderate philosophy would have throughout the country. At home there was the usual talk about a "dream ticket" and fond hopes of having a Tar Heel in the White House someday. Many in North Carolina hoped it was just a matter of time before the nation would think of their favorite son as the best alternative to other party names who had accumulated more baggage than anyone wished to carry into an election.

Kip Fowler had a profile right off a Roman frieze. Having been raised and educated in the East, he definitely did not speak like a typical southerner. He had unique personal mannerisms, gestures that many found positive. Some even thought inexplicably familiar. The right hand powerfully jabbing the podium during a speech. The penetrating, dark eyes. His rigid posture, and the way he confidently folded his hands on a desk when sparring with one of the Sunday morning political pundits.

Those traits were perceived as strong, definitely positive, and, yes, oddly familiar to those who had been active in North Carolina politics for many years. The young senator was unquestionably their man. His future had no limits in their way of thinking. But still there was something about Kip Fowler that made people wonder, but never quite understand. Somehow, he reminded them of someone. There was, however, one individual who knew all too well the answer to that riddle, the answer to the questions which were never asked. His name was Carter Burns.

CHAPTER 2

"I will. So help me God." With those solemn words, the Honorable Kent Reed, newly reelected mayor of Raleigh, vowed to uphold all that was great and just, and to faithfully serve the citizens of his city. Joining the mayor's wife, Charlotte, on the festively decorated inaugural stage were several dignitaries and special guests. They were dutifully enduring the cold wind and freezing temperatures on that January morning. Each person seated behind the speaker's podium was important to Mayor Reed, but none more important than his closest friend and advisor, Carter Burns.

A highly skilled and equally successful attorney, Burns considered Reed's entire political career as his own personal property. Within weeks of Reed's second inauguration as mayor, Burns was looking ahead to bigger things. Much bigger. On an unusually warm March afternoon, he first tried out his next political scheme for Raleigh's mayor. Burns and Marge Preston were walking on the beach at Hilton Head Island. He had flown to Savannah after taking two days of depositions in Atlanta and had caught the airport shuttle to Hilton Head, where he met his frequent companion. As many times before, she had driven down to the island from Raleigh a day or so earlier. There she waited for Burns to join her as soon as his schedule would permit. That had been their routine for more than three years. As far as she knew, that particular early spring trip was to be no different.

The wide, flat, almost concrete-like beach surrounding Hilton Head yielded few shells in the course of their walk and, initially little, if any, conversation between the two, who walked somewhat apart. Finally, Burns casually mentioned his plan for

Kent Reed's move to a higher political plateau. "I've been thinking about seeing if Kent would be interested in running for governor next time. What do you think?"

Knowing Burns always got what he went after, she was intrigued and welcomed the chance to talk about anything he might bring up, especially when he appeared to be so preoccupied. "Why, Kent?" she asked. "Why not Congressman Taylor? Taylor's been making noises about running for governor. You and Taylor have a good relationship. Don't you?"

"Bob Taylor and I have a great relationship. Always have. But if Kent announces soon enough, Bob will look elsewhere. He might even put his sights on Senator Mattox's seat. From what I hear, Mattox's wife's health is slipping. He should be about ready to retire. Prospects of a dynamic opponent like Taylor might just nudge him out of the picture gracefully. But Bob won't resist Kent, if Kent wants to run."

"But do you think Kent is ready to take on the entire state? A city race is one thing. North Carolina's a tad bit bigger. The issues are certainly different. Even I know that."

When she persisted in her doubts, Burns became defensive. "Marge, I damn well know Kent's up to it," he said flatly. "Don't forget. He'll have quite a few heavyweights behind him. He won't have any real problems that I can see. Raising the money will definitely be the biggest hurdle. It always is for any candidate. Planning and organization are the key factors, though."

"And that's where you come in, right?" Marge was well aware of his history with Kent Reed's political campaigns.

"I've floated the idea by Kent. He asked me to put together a few thoughts for him. We've already been putting a pencil to it."

She turned to look at him for the first time since the conversation began and out of curiosity asked, "And what's in it for you?"

"Well, counselor, that remains to be seen," he replied with a smile. "Can't say that a new challenge might not be tempting. The grind of a law practice isn't what it once was. You're an attorney.

You know how old it can get. It's just not as appealing as it once was. On the other hand, the governor appoints the attorney general. Now that has an appeal all its own."

"Isn't the attorney general just another attorney? Only maybe with a bigger stick?"

"My, aren't you the cynic today?" he said with not a little sarcasm. "No, the attorney general is not just the top attorney in the state. You might be surprised to know what crosses his desk any given day. There's the real power. The A.G. makes important decisions every day. Decisions that affect the lives of everyone in the state. That's quite a realm for anyone to control. Quite a choice plum for anyone to have in his grasp."

Marge realized Burns' mind was already set. What anyone else said did not matter. She moved closer to him as they walked and placed her arm around his waist. "And I'm sure that is just what will happen, kind sir. You'd make a fine attorney general." She mused out loud. "General Burns. Sounds like some Confederate general leading a charge up some hill."

"Marge, I believe that was General Burn*side*," he corrected her and laughed.

Burns was always precise about everything. He had a well-earned reputation for taking care of the most minute details. Reed's campaign for governor would be no different. "In any situation, you can't leave any questions unasked or any turn of events unanticipated. All possible scenarios have to be looked at and thoroughly evaluated. Kent will most certainly have Republican opposition. That can't be ignored. He might even have to face Stewart Harris, if Harris runs as an Independent like he's threatening to do, since the Democratic Executive Committee didn't appoint his man state party chairman. Harris might even take a lot of maverick Democrats with him if he did that. But I seriously doubt he'll bolt the party. We'll probably have to face him in the primary."

A recently admitted member of the Raleigh Bar Association herself, Marge wondered how such an extensive campaign would affect Burns' law practice. She was very familiar with the work habits of successful attorneys. Her late husband had been an attorney and an adversarial colleague of Carter Burns for many years. Each man had been married to his career. But in many ways she knew they were different. Her husband had been a bookish slave to his clients. On the other hand, Burns was no one's slave. He was more in control of his life and everything around him. Burn set a fast pace others had to follow, always in one direction, toward one goal—power—the precious commodity Carter Burns valued above all else and at all costs.

In her private thoughts, Marge often compared her husband with Burns in other, more personal ways. Wendell Preston had been five-feet seven-inches tall and constantly needed to diet. Burns was slightly over six feet and had a steel stomach. Wendell Preston had hard-to-control graying hair, while Burns' dark brown preppy cut was always in place. Her husband had the sex drive of a veteran of the Spanish-American War, while in that department Burns resembled a Kentucky thoroughbred and handled it with the finesse of a porn star. At that point in her mental exercise, Marge always grinned and felt a slight twitch in her stomach. At age forty-four she felt positive about herself and her life, particularly since it included having Carter Burns as a frequent guest on Hilton Head, where she and her older sister owned a condominium she had helped finance with part of her husband's life insurance proceeds.

Eventually, their walk took them to the bar at the lighthouse in Harbor Towne, a favorite shopping area on the island. Not seeing a hostess, they proceeded upstairs. Finding their usual booth vacant, they quickly claimed it, although the bar was relatively empty for that time of the day. "Carter, look. That sunset looks like a painting," Marge remarked as she slid into the red vinyl booth. A brilliant orange sun streaked the water between the deepening shadows on the restless bay. Begging sea gulls circled the boats drawn up to the graying dock. "Carter, look at those two kids." She pointed out the window at two small boys running down the dockside proudly carrying a string of equally small fish. "Now that's a Norman Rockwell moment if there ever was one," she warmly observed.

But Burns was not interested in the view. "I need to make a telephone call. Order me a double Scotch on the rocks," he said, as he removed his crew neck sweater and tossed it into the booth beside her. "I'll be right back." With that he went downstairs to use the pay telephone.

When he returned after about five minutes, his drink was waiting. "Have you heard a forecast?" he asked, as he took his seat across from her. "Those clouds look like one of those sudden spring storms might be heading this way."

Marge looked up from her own bourbon and water. She was relieved to sense his tone was lighter than in their earlier conversation. "No, I haven't had the radio or the television on all day. But you're probably right. Those can come up so quickly here. We'd better go back. I want to wash this hair before dinner. You seem like you could use a nap," she suggested. Her raven hair was tied back with a large red bandanna, revealing only a short, stubby ponytail. "I never understand it. But the salt air makes my hair feel like straw. It happens every time, even if I cover it up."

"I think you're right about those clouds. Let's head back," he said, quickly downing his drink. "Something's brewing out there for sure. But who cares? We're not having to worry about a boat, and even a hurricane beats taking those damn depositions in Atlanta."

"Is that what you told your wife?" she asked, as they reached the outside. "That you're taking depositions all this time?"

"Marge, why do you always say my 'wife'? You know Florence. You've met her a dozen times at Bar Association functions. Why don't you just say 'Florence'? I always refer to Wendell as 'Wendell'." He tried to be light about it, but mentioning his wife and his personal life struck a nerve.

"When he was alive, he called you more than one name," she said laughing, trying to keep the conversation light. "And it wasn't always 'Carter.' Gracious, he hated you sometimes."

He was genuinely taken back by her disclosure. "Hated me? I thought Wendell and I got along fairly well. Especially after I helped elect him president of the Bar Association," he noted indignantly.

"Well, maybe not hate, but he did think you were arrogant. Something of an ass, I believe he said," she teased. She enjoyed seeing him defensive and the attention she was getting. Feeling adventuresome, she decided to take advantage of the moment and see if he would tell her what was troubling him. "You seem preoccupied. You have been all afternoon. Is something bothering you? It's really not the case you're working on, is it?"

"There's just a lot going on. You must know that. It's probably the campaign. What we were talking about earlier," he offered.

"This one will mean a lot to you, won't it."

"Damn right it will! And it's going to take a hell of a lot of my time. This election's the key to the next twenty years in politics in North Carolina. Politics seem to run in ten- or even twenty-year increments. *Cycles* is probably a better word. I'm convinced this is the beginning of one of those cycles. Anyone who doesn't understand will damn well be left behind when the train leaves. You can bet on that one."

His reference to time reminded her of her own needs. "I wish you didn't have to go back tomorrow. You've only been here such a short time. Couldn't you stay at least one more day? I'm sure Mary could cover for you, if you asked her." She referred to his long-time secretary, who had made a vocation out of covering for her boss over the years.

"I can't. I have that meeting with Kent tomorrow on city business. We've got a couple of things that've been pending for weeks and won't wait any longer. How long do you plan to stay this trip?"

"Sis is coming down whenever I call her, but I should be back in the office by the end of the week. She never stays long this time of year."

As they walked down the tree-lined street toward her condominium, another couple passed them on bicycles, followed by two laughing children being dragged by a large Irish setter on a long leash. Dodging the dog and the children, she returned to what was on her mind. "I know Kent is a friend of yours. But this election seems so much more important than anything I've heard you talk about for some time. Why is that?"

Still walking, he replied, "Marge, I've spent too many days, too many years in fancy conference rooms taking depositions. Listening to half-bright lawyers carry the art of bullshitting to new heights. I've had it with incompetent judges and stubborn, demanding clients. I want more now. Not more of the same. That's for damn sure. Not by a long shot. I don't intend to spend the next twenty years or even twenty months filing motions and solving other people's screw-ups."

"And being named attorney general will do the trick?"

"I think so."

"Sounds like you've got it all worked out. Just like everything else you do," she said with a note of resentment she tried unsuccessfully to suppress. "I'll bet you decided at age fourteen that you would become a rich and famous lawyer. At age twenty-one or twenty-two, maybe, that you would be the best in the business. And now you've decided to be the top dog. The *numero uno* attorney in all of North Carolina," she said, adding with some sarcasm, "and you do have a record of getting exactly what you want."

Burns did not want an argument, so he avoided her tone. "The answer to all your questions is a qualified 'yes.' But you're slightly wrong about a few of the details. At age fourteen I decided to become captain of the football team, which I eventually did. I didn't decide to become an attorney until I was at least twenty-one and being the best was never a question at all," he said with a mocking laugh. He glanced over to catch her expression, hoping she would get off the subject. But she merely stared ahead as they walked the final blocks to her home.

Eventually, she asked, "And what happens when you're the A.G.? That's a pretty tight schedule, I would imagine. Those guys just don't get away easily. God knows it's difficult enough for you even now. Will I be supposed to make an appointment with the busy man just like all the others?"

Before he could reply, they reached the gate to the enclosed patio of her condominium. The walk back from the bar at Harbor Towne had taken about fifteen minutes. Still there was no sign of the storm, but they were glad to make it back without getting drenched, as had happened once before. Marge quickly unlocked the front door, while Burns latched the patio gate behind them. "I'm going to wash this mop," she reminded him. She snatched the bandanna off her head and disappeared up the stairs to her bedroom.

Once behind the closed bathroom door, she turned on the full lights surrounding the mirror over the lavatory. First tossing the bandanna, then the rest of her clothes into the wicker hamper, she turned and stood before the full-length mirror on the back of the bathroom door. She looked at her high cheek-bones and saw only faint crow's feet. What the hell, she thought, I've earned them. She saw the reddish appendectomy scar she had had since she was nineteen, and couldn't avoid the Cesarean scar from the birth on her only child. Her son, Jason, was a college senior majoring in journalism and considering law school. Pleased, she muttered, "At least my butt's not sagging yet." Then she stepped quickly into the steaming shower, only to emerge several minutes later feeling much better and definitely in need of affection.

Wrapping her pale blue cotton robe around her, she opened the bathroom door and stepped into the bedroom. She towel-dried her hair as she looked to the bed, expecting to find Burns, perhaps taking a nap. But he was not there waiting for her as he always did. Walking to the top of the staircase, she listened. She could hear Burns talking on the telephone downstairs. She listened just long enough to realize he was talking with his office. She dressed slowly, contemplating whatever was happening. Recapping the day, Marge was not sure about many things at that point, but something was different, of that she was convinced.

Allowing Burns a few more minutes to finish his call, she went downstairs but saw he was still on the telephone. She walked into the kitchen, then turned to ask if his favorite shepherd's pie and tossed salad would be okay, but Burns never looked up from his conversation. It would be the first time they had been on Hilton Head without making love.

Burns was up earlier than usual the next morning. After taking a shower, he confirmed he had to get back to Raleigh. "I had Mary book me an earlier flight out of Savannah. You don't need to drive me. I'll just catch the airport shuttle at the Hilton. Besides, it's beginning to rain."

"No, Carter, I want to drive you. It's no problem," she assured him, as she got out of bed and began getting dressed. She felt confused and gave into a need to make things better somehow. "Sorry I've been such a bitch. I won't bring up anything unpleasant again. No questions. Promise. You have my professional word on that, counselor," she reluctantly said in jest. She did not share her gnawing fear that this would be his last trip for a long time. If not forever, troubled her even more.

CHAPTER 3

The late March weather was exceptionally warm for Raleigh. Too eager gardeners had to be admonished by weather forecasters. "Go ahead and till your flower beds. But keep your hands away from seeds and bedding plants. We still have dogwood winter to go through." Nothing, however, could damper the enthusiasm of those addicted to hitting a small white ball with a sleek, metal headed stick over immaculate green islands, each one bearing a single small hole of destiny.

The moderately stiff breeze merely served as the siren's song promising a lower handicap to golfing members of the exclusive Brookside Country Club. They were anxiously lined up at every tee. Founded in 1926 in what eventually developed into Raleigh's most prestigious residential area, Brookside Country Club was considered the unrivaled Mecca for the privileged few who achieved membership, often with the assistance of a well-to-do father or, as in many cases, father-in-law. For decades Raleigh's rich powerbrokers gathered faithfully at "The Club," as it was reverently referred to in North Raleigh's fashionable living rooms and in warmly paneled boardrooms downtown. Those occasions, big and small, determined the fate of bank loans, corporate mergers, local political candidates, and any type of deal in which there was a dollar to be made or career to be massaged. Out of primeval necessity, players carefully protected their own turf, both business and personal.

In North Raleigh, a young wife's entire life often centered around meetings of the Junior League and giddy luncheons at Brookside. Failure to attain either of those pinnacles exiled a budding society matron to years of servitude in any number of organizations patronized by the non-League members, and reduced not just a few to clawing to get their names mentioned as often as possible in the Sunday newspaper's gossip column.

And then there were the husbands. Acceptance in North Raleigh circles depended on a young man's preferably having been born there and having attended Duke University. If his bloodlines could not be traced immediately to North Raleigh, a young man needed to have married, at least the first time, a young woman whose parents were part of the good-old-boy and good-old-gal network. Any combination of those criteria meant success. But the essential requirement was a "daddy" on one side or the other of the marriage who could open doors and, when necessary, squelch talk following a night of too much vodka and skinny dipping in the club pool or the pond just off the seventh green.

There were, however, a few notable exceptions to the typical profile of a Brookside member. A self-made man was a rare commodity in that environment. And Carter Burns was one such exception. He was leaving the Gentlemen's Grill on that balmy March afternoon the day after his return from Hilton Head Island. In the hallway he encountered his older friend Wink Collins. Both men were heading toward the locker room for a quick shower and change of clothes.

"How'd you shoot?" Burns asked, as he gave Collins a slap on his butt.

"Not too shabby for an old man," Collins responded. "My game's still rough after spending so much time on that damn trial. That kind of ordeal takes a lot out of a man. Any man."

"Sure it does, Wink. But you've got to put that behind you now. The sooner the better. It's over. Finished." Burns was referring to the past eighteen months he had spent extracting Collins from the scrutiny of a recently-appointed United States Attorney obviously intent on making a name for himself. As the sole owner and chief executive officer of Collins Construction Company, Wink Collins had been accused of participating in a widespread bid-rigging scheme involving interstate bridge construction contracts. The scandal and the resulting fine cost Collins his business and a major portion of his wealth. In exchange for his testimony against other construction contractors, Collins's sentence had been suspended by the court. But the hefty fine dealt him a severe blow, and the loss of the business robbed him of his only opportunity to recoup his loss easily. However, the biggest blow had been to his pride and the fragile emotional health of his wife, Ellen. As a past president of Brookside Country Club, Collins enjoyed a lifetime membership without dues. But socially the Collinses remained in a shadow.

"Oh, hell, Carter, I can take it. I've had it bad before. Nothing like this, mind you. But Ellen's got a real problem. This thing's nearly killed her. It's all I can do to drag her out of the house. The ordeal may be over, but the tongues are still wagging, and that eats at her day and night."

Inside the locker room, Burns sat down on a bench in front of his locker. He quickly removed his shoes and socks, then took a long drink of the beer he had brought from the grill. "I know this has taken a toll on Ellen. It'll probably take some time before she fully gets out from under this. But you know how this town is. If you're accused of anything short of murder or child molesting, they talk about you for about two weeks and then quickly move on to the next hot topic. Worse things have happened to people. You know who I'm talking about. And they still thrive among us with their heads held high. People forget quicker than you and Ellen might think. Hell, forgiving has nothing to do with it either. No one bothers. They don't really give a shit. They just forget. Period. Then it's over."

"Easier said than done, my friend," Collins said. "But I'm sure you're right. You always have been where I'm concerned."

"Let me ask you something, Wink." Burns wanted to get off the subject and move on to what had been on his mind since he first ran into Collins outside the grill. "The mayor needs to appoint someone to fill that vacancy on the Raleigh Board of Health. I was thinking about recommending that he appoint your son-in-law. Do you think Ken might be interested in something like that?" Burns was referring to Dr. Kenneth Harmon, who had established his plastic surgery practice in Raleigh two years before. The vacancy on the Board of Health had resulted from the retirement of a prominent neurosurgeon, and that slot on the board had traditionally been held by a surgeon.

Collins took another swallow of his own beer, as he considered Burns' proposal. "Of course, I'm sure Ken would be interested, Carter. He seems to have quite an interest in the community. But you've done enough lately. You really have. It isn't necessary for you or Wedge to do that. It really isn't."

"I'm not just doing it for you, Wink," Burns assured him. "Sure, you've done a hell of a lot for the mayor in the past, but this vacancy calls for a surgeon. It's been open since Dr. Allen's retirement. We want to fill it as soon as possible. Besides, Ken's impressed a lot of people with his activities at the Children's Hospital. Hell, he single-handedly made the Rehabilitation Center's marathon the success it was. Those young kids benefited greatly from the first rate job he did." Burns stood up and pulled his cotton sweater and shirt over his head. Unfastening his belt, he continued to pursue his objective. "Ken's got a great deal to offer. I think the board can put that energy to good use."

"No doubt about what Ken's got to offer. He's a fine doctor. One of the best. My daughter's a lucky girl. We're all lucky to have him in the family."

"I think Raleigh's fortunate, too, Wink. Do you think Caroline would mind sharing him with the board?"

"Of course not, Carter. It's a terrific idea. I'm sure they'll both be pleased you thought of them."

Wrapping a towel around his waist, Burns appreciated Collins's reaction. "Great. I'm seeing Wedge later today. I'll tell him we've talked. He can contact Ken first thing Monday."

Both men continued to talk as they showered, but only about their golf games. Each felt there had been enough serious discussion for that afternoon. After shaving for the second time that day, Burns put on his standard navy blue blazer, white Polo shirt, and pleated gray slacks. On his way out of the club, he stopped to check with his caddie again about having his clubs cleaned before the following day's match. His next destination was his office for the meeting with Kent "Wedge" Reed, two-term mayor of Raleigh, long-time friend, and, if Burns had his way, North Carolina's next chief executive.

CHAPTER 4

The law office of Burns and Walters occupied the entire eighteenth and part of the seventeenth floors of the First National Bank of Raleigh building, commonly referred to as the "First Nasty" building. That was attributable to the bank's reputation for dealing roughly with nonpedigreed customers and even a few of the city's elite who were unfortunate enough to fall from favor with Harlan Dandridge, Chairman of the Board of First National, himself a symbol of Raleigh's "old money," which had controlled the city's largest bank since well before World War II.

Carter Burns savored the prestige offered by having his offices in the bank building, where he allowed only one other name on the firm's letterhead, as well as on the mahogany double doors to the suite. That name belonged to Seth Walters, who similarly felt at home in the heavily Brookside-enclave atmosphere of the law firm, and in many other offices housed at 400 Beacon Street. The two lawyers even liked the nickname "First Nasty." Burns was fond of saying that "if you have that reputation, you probably have the money and power to back it up." That thought suited Burns and Walters very nicely indeed.

Despite the lack of a string of names on the door, the firm of Burns and Walters was quite large by North Carolina standards. Among the thirty-two attorneys, Burns took considerable pride in attracting top law school graduates, preferably from schools in the South. "They need to be smart as hell and still talk like we do" was his rationale. While the junior members of the firm were paid good salaries, all the fame and glory belonged to the two senior partners. Burns insisted on leaving any mentoring chores to

Walters, and each junior member was assigned a week at a time to polish the large bronze letters on the entrance doors to the suite after hours. The senior partner considered it a not-too-subtle reminder of "where they are and who's in charge."

Burns had made his reputation when he worked as the youngest-ever United States Attorney for the eastern district of North Carolina. He had ruthlessly prosecuted major crime figures in the late 1960s, often delegating little of the work to other attorneys in the office and seldom missing the opportunity to take the credit for "doing the people's work," as he described his mission. Early on, he attracted the idol-worshipping Seth Walters and saw the value of the younger man because of Walter's workaholic tendencies and willingness to stay in the background. The only morsel Burns cast toward Seth Walters was putting Walter's name on the door. There the special treatment ended abruptly. The stable of attorneys at Burns and Walters was ridden hard. Anyone who did not carry their share of the work load was soon looking for employment elsewhere. At Burns and Walters, families did not count. Each attorney was expected to marry the firm and passionately embrace the legal profession. All other aspects of life were at best secondary, even nonexistent. After all, they worked at Burns and Walters, where the practice of law was considered mother's milk, if an attorney's head was screwed on right.

While the main suite of the firm's offices was on the eighteenth floor of the bank building, the library and copy room operations were located on the seventeenth floor, along with the small and seldom-used break area. Each attorney was assigned a private carrel in the library to be used for research purposes. One carrel had a brass plaque fastened on the front of the desk reading "In Memory of Evan Potter Hayden. United States Senator. Statesman and Attorney." That particular carrel was always assigned to the ranking associate and had been so designated by Burns, who had served as an aide to the senator after graduating top of his class from Duke University School of Law. Unlike most top graduates, Burns's talent was not bookish. He hadn't even been considered by many to be the smartest in his class. But everyone knew the aggressive Burns just worked harder.

There was only one other office for the firm located on the seventeenth floor. That sequestered space belonged exclusively to Carter Burns himself. For normal business purposes, he maintained a magnificent office on the eighteenth floor with all the others. There he had the obligatory diplomas and licenses, as well as framed letters from famous jurists and politicians and awards from various bar associations. On his desk was a family photograph of Burns with his wife and a young girl in pigtails holding a blonde cocker spaniel puppy. On a pedestal in one corner of the room was a marble Roman bust he had acquired at an auction in Europe, along with other carefully selected items intended to render his clients awestruck. His collection of eagles was something else: prints of eagles by important artists, bronze statues of eagles in flight, and an eagle carved from fossilized whale bone by an ancient Alaskan artisan. All seemed to swirl around the richly appointed room over which the attorney proudly presided. He was particularly fond of the bronze plaque on the top of his desk. It read "Eagles Fly Alone."

By contrast, Burns's office on the seventeenth floor was very private. In the firm, only Seth Walters was ever allowed in that sacred space, and then only on the rare occasions when Burns summoned him. The door remained locked at all times with only Burns and his personal secretary having keys. The room was only cleaned when she was present. Burns coveted the privacy afforded by the location on the seventeenth floor. By entering through a private, unmarked entrance, he could be in his office without anyone knowing he was present. Only Mary Cole, his trusted secretary of many years, would be told by Burns whenever he arrived that he was in his private sanctum.

In many respects, the two offices were essentially the same. Eagles gazed from various vantage points. And the rich, autumnal colors he preferred were dominant. However, there were notable differences on the seventeenth floor. Gilt-framed oil paintings, one by an Impressionist master. An exquisite tapestry from

Venice, and ship replicas dating back to sixteenth-century England. The richly upholstered chairs matched the antique Chinese rug. It was all very fine and very valuable, representing the man's keenly drawn self-image. That private world reflected a taste Carter Burns had acquired later in life. There had been none of that growing up in western North Carolina poor, but determined.

Growing up, he had never known what status actually meant in the larger world outside his small hometown. He never knew the finer things money could buy, because there had been no money in the first place. His family had none of the trappings he came to admire. Being captain of the high school football team had been status enough. However, all that changed, and so did Carter Burns. Attending college on a work scholarship, he learned quickly what he wanted in life, what he wanted to own, how to acquire it. The office on the seventeenth floor became Burns' personal monument to his success. On the eighteenth floor, he shared his glory with the world. On the floor below, he seldom shared anything. There he reveled in the trappings he coveted, each one a symbol of accomplishment and power—in his mind, the ultimate object.

After leaving Brookside and his friend Wink, Carter Burns drove his black Lincoln Town Car into his reserved parking space in the bank building's garage just before noon. When he got out, he noticed the mayor's unmarked Caprice parked in a space reserved by Burns for friends and special clients. He knew Kent Reed would be waiting for him in the office on the eighteenth floor, probably working on his second or third cup of coffee, depending on how long he had been waiting, and probably using Burns's private telephone line. Instead, Burns took the service elevator to the seventeenth floor. Even on a Saturday, someone he might not want to encounter could be on the public elevators, and he preferred not to waste his time.

He went quickly to the unmarked door, let himself in, and walked down the empty hallway to his private office. Walking to his desk, he buzzed Mary Cole and told her to send Kent Reed down to where he was. He also asked for a cup of coffee, which Reed could bring himself. Within five minutes, Kent Reed, mayor of Raleigh, was standing before Burns's desk, handing him his coffee as directed. Before either spoke, Reed walked over to the wet bar and put a shot of expensive brandy in his own cup. He raised the bottle, motioning to ask whether Burns wanted the same, but the attorney shook his head, declining.

Reed was the first to speak. "Frankly, I didn't expect to see you here today. Didn't think you'd show. I just came over to get away and to use your telephone without the usual interruptions." He was looking over his coffee cup at Burns, who was leafing through a stack of papers his secretary had placed on his desk before he arrived.

"Why was that?" Burns asked, without looking up. He reached for his briefcase, which was standing on the floor beside the desk.

"Hell, Carter. Because of Marge" was Reed's bewildered response. He was referring to Marge Preston. It had been reported in the morning newspapers that she died the day before. Authorities in South Carolina determined that she had lost control of her automobile on the rain-slick highway between the Savannah Airport and Hilton Head Island. Returning from the airport, she had rammed head-on into a concrete overpass support at a high rate of speed.

"Yes, I know all about that, Wedge. The firm will send flowers" was the only comment Burns made as he placed some more papers into his briefcase. He closed it and looked up at Reed for the first time.

"Is that all you have to say? Carter, I don't quite believe you. For three fucking years . . ."

Burns cut him off in mid-sentence. "Wedge, the less about that the better, old buddy."

Reed looked off and then back at Burns. "Carter, as long as I've known you, I've known you can be one cold son of a bitch when you want to. But this tops everything. You know that?

You're acting like Marge was just another member of the damned Bar Association to you."

"As far as anyone else knows, that is precisely the case, my friend. And it will stay that way. I may be a son of a bitch, but, as I see it right now, that seems to be in your favor. Especially now. You know I don't mix my private life with business. Period. Okay? And you make sure my private life is kept just that—private," Burns warned. "Marge is part of the past. Even she knew that. Believe me."

Reed realized it was time to retreat. "Sure thing, counselor. But I just can't see how a man . . ."

Again Burns broke in. "That's how it is, Wedge. All anyone knows or ever will know is that she and I were fellow attorneys. That's the sum total of it." The subject was closed.

In a matter-of-fact, almost professorial tone, Burns began outlining his thoughts about the upcoming campaign for governor in which Reed would be the star and Burns would be the ultimate driving force. Reed sat and listened dutifully as the master laid it all out for him piece by piece.

Burns had determined that it was time for Kent Reed to seek the office of governor of North Carolina, and several influential backers of the mayor agreed without question. As always in the past, Reed went along with his friends and their plans. He always had. They were confident he always would. His closest associates called him "Wedge," a nickname he acquired in his college football days, a time when Good Old Wedge needed a strong coach. In Burns he needed another one for the governor's race. Burns would call every play from the not-too-distant sidelines. The two men had been close since college, when Burns also gave his friend directions more than once.

"Most insiders think your opponent in the primary will be Stewart Harris. That's the general consensus, at this juncture at least. It could change. But I don't think so. I don't see anyone out there willing to jump in at this time." Harris was the oldest son of the late former governor Vernon Harris. "As his father's son, Stewart is heir to a great deal of affection and respect which I, frankly, think he little deserves in his own right. He's shallow and overbearing as hell. A poor imitation of his dad, but that's what he will try to portray himself as—Vernon Harris reincarnated. But it won't work, in my opinion. Nevertheless, Stewart can do no wrong in the eyes of those who remember the good old days and want like hell to run the state again. They miss being on the public tit. They screwed the state for many years and are very willing to screw it again with Stewart's blessings."

Burns continued, as Reed listened attentively, taking mental notes. "That's one thing we can hang on old Stew. The 'same old crowd' tag. Unless I miss my guess, he's going to surround himself with his father's political retreads. Might even be forced to, if I know that crowd correctly. But we don't want to have the same liability laid on us. Your campaign's going to have a new look, project a new day for North Carolina. A lot of people, Bryce Talmadge for one, will have to be content with staying in the background as much as possible. At least during the campaign. Afterward will be another matter, but we'll cross that bridge when we get to it. We can't afford to offend them, but we sure as hell can't have you look like the hand-picked candidate of a single segment of the party. We'll need fresh faces out front in this thing."

Burns walked to the single office window and continued his dialogue. "Our biggest problem will be money, but that's a factor in any campaign, particularly at first when people are still trying to gauge which way the winds are blowing. It's going to take quite a bit of the stuff to make you as well known in the entire state as you are here in Raleigh. Campaign treasurer is one of the most visible positions to fill. Certainly the most sensitive. Talmadge will do whatever is needed, just as he has for everyone since John Kennedy in 1960." Stamping his foot and turning to face Reed, Burns said, "Christ, I wish I had that man's contacts. But we've got to have a new face in the treasurer's spot. The best of both worlds—Talmadge's money sources and a certifiable saint making all the photo opportunities." He was sensitive to

Talmadge's other, less attractive qualities, which were not common knowledge in Raleigh.

Burns was emphatic and understood the wisdom of all he had shared with his friend. He only hoped his audience of one did as well. But he knew it really didn't matter. Whether Reed did or not, he would go along with the game plan no matter what.

Next followed more of Campaign 101. "We've got to concentrate on naming the right person to that position and several others. Someone with all the right credentials, the right appearance. Someone who is willing, nonetheless, to let us call the shots from here." Reed walked over to the wet bar for another shot of brandy, as he listened patiently, while his tutor laid it all out for him as he had so many times before. He never interrupted. Asked no questions. He understood all too well that the answers would be forthcoming.

Finally, Burns asked one. "Do you have any suggestions on treasurer?"

"No, I haven't really given it much thought at this point. From where I sit, it sounds like you might have someone in mind already." He knew Burns would never ask a question without having his own answer ready.

"Do you know Greg Barlow?" Burns asked, confirming Reed's suspicion. "Greg's an attractive, ambitious guy from what I've observed at Bar Association meetings. He gets around and probably wants to get around even more. This might be his first time out in the political wars, so he certainly should be clean. What do you think about my approaching him? See if he has any interests in politics at all."

"Go ahead, Carter. You know I trust your judgment on these things. Your instincts are usually right on the mark. Have you spoken with Bob Henry about running the headquarters operations? You mentioned wanting to see if he was available."

Henry was a young, street-smart stockbroker who had worked in several smaller campaigns, including Stewart Harris's reelection to the State Board of Claims. Early on, he had been considered by Reed's backers as ideal for the mayor's gubernatorial team, particularly with Henry's knowledge of the Harris political machinery. "The rumor in some circles is that Henry's dissatisfied with Stewart Harris because he didn't appoint him to any position after Harris's successful campaign two years earlier," Burns explained.

"As a matter of fact, I did discuss it with him, but only briefly. Just to plant the idea in his head. I called him before I went to Atlanta last week." It was obvious to Reed that the reference was to Atlanta, not to Hilton Head. "He's all for it. At least that was his initial reaction. He's confident he can get a leave of absence from work. With pay, I might add. And that's important to us. That's money we can spend elsewhere." Burns never missed an angle or an opportunity.

"By the way," Burns added. "Guess who's going to run the Harris campaign? At least from the scuttlebutt I've heard so far."

"Not Andrew Denson?"

"None other. And that's from a reliable source."

"I can't believe they'd trot out that hack again. Denson has all the tact of a wounded rhino," Reed almost shouted. Andy Denson, a high school dropout, had been Stewart Harris's father's campaign manager his last term and had served as Commissioner of Highways at one point and later as Commissioner of Pubic Works in Vernon Harris's cabinet. "Denson has all the administrative know-how of a Cub Scout working on a merit badge in nuclear engineering."

"Old Andy hasn't had a new idea in about thirty years. No, make that forty. About anything," Burns said with no little contempt.

"Have you got anything on him?" Reed had to ask. Burns kept a mental file on all members of the opposition, no matter how small the battle. At that point the two men resembled fraternity brothers planning a panty raid. "Surely, he can't be all that clean after being involved with the Harris crowd all these years. Maybe we can dig up some pictures with Andy and Stewart's Aunt Louise involved in something other than talking politics." Both laughed at the prospect.

"I hate to admit it, but even Andy Denson has more taste than that," Burns said begrudgingly. "But that would be one hell of a sight. God, Wedge, you're more evil than I thought." And they both chuckled again.

Louise Harris Coleman, a steel gray, self-styled dragon lady, had run her brother Vernon's last administration. She was the butt of many jokes in the Tar Heel State—by those who dared to do so. It had been said that the nine-foot stuffed polar bear in the State Museum was the offspring of Louise and a once powerful lobbyist who had loved to hunt. Eventually, the story had been revised, making the poor bear Louise's clone. The woman was slightly over six feet tall, and revisionists thought better about the lobbyist's taste.

Returning to his desk from the window, Burns remarked, "That's all we need to cover right now, as far as I'm concerned, Wedge. I'm meeting with Hardwick in about two weeks. I may have already told you that. Are all the bases covered on that one?" He was referring to the award of the city government's insurance program to one of the five agencies that had bid on the lucrative project.

"Everything's in place, Carter. One more insurance company than expected submitted a bid. But I made sure no one came close. At least, too close to Hardwick's. I don't think anyone except Hardwick could meet the specifications as written." The city's purchasing director had personally seen to that at the mayor's instructions. "Arnie Cox knew what he was doing and what he was supposed to do. He's delivered many times before."

"Keep your distance as much as you can. But don't let it get away from us. Cox is good, but he still needs to be watched," Burns warned.

"I know what to do. Arnie's reliable. He won't let anything slip or get by him. He never has. He won't start with this one. He knows it's sensitive."

"Good. Give him my regards once the thing's over. By the way, go ahead and contact Ken Harmon about that medical board slot. I discussed it with Wink. He said it sounded like a good idea."

But Reed had one more question. "With Stewart Harris in this thing, what about the Fowler people? They've been pretty tight in the past."

Burns wasted no time responding. "Leave the Fowlers to me. At the right time, I'll approach Lenore with the facts of life. That's all it will take. If nothing else, I've got that one covered."

"If it's that easy, you damn well must have something on the great lady herself."

"All you need to know is that the Fowlers will not be a factor in this race. And that's enough said on that particular subject." He felt a need to add a warning. "And don't bring that subject up, if we're with anyone else. The less said, the better. Just leave it to me."

Sensing the meeting was over, Reed placed his empty cup in the sink at the wet bar. Both men agreed to keep in constant touch over the next several days and to keep their regular raquetball time the following evening at the Brookside Country Club where Reed was Burns's frequent guest. Their close relationship was well known in Raleigh, but both preferred to keep some of their private meetings just that—private—so Reed left by the service elevator. That way there would be fewer questions to answer.

CHAPTER 5

His friend Reed barely had time to get on the elevator before Burns looked at the quartz Seiko clock and then back to the stack of mail and messages. He realized that, if he was going to get anything accomplished from that point on, he would need the brandy he quickly poured at the well-stocked wet bar across the room from his desk. It was only four o'clock, but the day and its events, Reed had reminded him of so forcefully, had taken a toll. He viewed plotting and scheming as hard work, often requiring fortification, even as razor sharp as his plotting and scheming skills were from years of practice. A snifter of expensive brandy often took the edge off, allowing Burns to concentrate on the comparatively mundane office matters represented by the clutter on his desk and the small mountain in the walnut "in" basket, courtesy of Mrs. Cole.

One particular telephone message caused him to pick up the brandy and pensively lean back in his chair. The message was on the standard telephone message pad and noted that Jean Talmadge had called the day before, when he was in Hilton Head. The caller had asked that he phone her back as soon as possible on a number which was clearly designated as "unlisted" on the message slip.

Jean Talmadge was the former daughter-in-law of Bryce T. Talmadge, a powerful political ally Burns carefully cultivated, but kept at arm's length. Bryce Talmadge had a tendency to be possessive about some people, particularly those who were collectively referred to around Raleigh as "Bryce's boys." Jean had been married to Warren Talmadge, Bryce's oldest son and a prominent insurance executive. Warren was noted for being less interested in the insurance business than in his father's financial empire—and cocaine. Jean was thirty-three and, in Burns' opinion, one great looking natural blonde. She had called him and left her private number.

Burns contemplated the message a moment longer and then decided to wait until Monday to return the call. If the jet-setting former Mrs. Warren Talmadge needed him, he decided, she would just have to wait a little longer. He was confident she would not call another attorney, even Jean Burkes Talmadge, former daughter-in-law of the most powerful money-raiser and one of the wealthiest people in the entire mid-Atlantic region, perhaps even in every place south of the old Mason-Dixon line. And he was even more certain that, if she had called, her former father-in-law would not be far behind, something Burns preferred to avoid whenever possible.

As he backed out of his parking space in the First National Bank of Raleigh building, Burns saw that it was almost six o'clock. He would be getting home later than normal for a Saturday and with one, actually two, more brandies than usual under his belt. Out of habit he switched on the car radio, only to be confronted again by the news of the death of Marge Preston.

Instantly turning off the radio, he continued thinking about the woman he had left at the airport in Savannah the day before. Perhaps, he acknowledged to himself, he had been thinking about her most of the day. The suddenly abrupt silence in the car reminded him of their conversation between Hilton Head Island and the Savannah terminal. As he had driven her Audi 5000, that conversation too began, or at least intensified when she switched off the radio and asked him why he pushed himself and even others as hard as he did.

After spending the previous several hours cautiously avoiding a confrontation, his reply to her question was aggressive, somewhat defensive. All to be expected from someone wholly unaccustomed to being questioned about anything, much less himself or his motives, whatever the subject. Carter Burns asked questions, and he was a master. He did not answer them readily.

Gradually, as he drove toward Savannah, his mood changed and deepened, even without additional coaxing. His thoughts went further back than even his inquiring companion had expected.

Actually, the normally cocksure attorney was somewhat curious about the thoughts he had been having about himself over the previous weeks. At first he had attributed the flashbacks to a midlife crisis type of thing. But the frequency and depth of them established a presence of their own in his consciousness. To himself he acknowledged that, indeed, he was at a pivotal point in his life. Particularly where his career was concerned. No longer content with wooing a jury or browbeating opposing counsel, he realized he needed more. But more of what? Power was the conclusion he had come to with surprising ease. Power would be what he sought in everything he did from that time forward, as if he had not been doing just that for quite some time.

Without looking at his companion, he drove even faster, despite the increasing rain aggressively peppering the windshield. Finally, Burns was willing to offer an answer with relative calm, considering the mood he was in. "You'd probably laugh if I said I push myself because there's nothing else. Getting there, the battle is everything. Much more important and, to me, satisfying than even reaching the goal, whatever it might be at the moment. I just enjoy a good fight. Plain and simple."

He reflected on what he had said for a second and then continued. Recalling his youth in Burke County, he said, "I've always had to prove myself. At school in athletics and in practically everything else, because there was little or no recognition or attention at home. The bottom line was that I never thought that anyone—anyone really close to me that should have—really gave a damn about me or anything I did." He started to apologize for sounding melodramatic, but resisted sounding weak, even to his lover.

Although hating to interrupt, Marge asked, "Why did you feel that way? Were you just completely ignored? Did someone ever flat out say you didn't matter?"

At that point his tone changed. Burns tersely elaborated, perhaps for the first time to anyone. "No, of course not. It was just that my parents were too damned absorbed in their own petty problems to give me the time of day. My father worked as an insurance salesman and had, for as long as I could remember, put up with a wife who was never satisfied with anything. Nothing had been good enough for my mother. As a kid, I primarily grew up left alone in many ways, almost entirely on my own. I looked for recognition from friends early on. Later, I guess I looked to sports rivals, teachers, anyone. But, as I see it now, that required first making everything a contest and everyone an adversary. Each one to be challenged and beaten and, consequently, won over, I suppose. There were no exceptions. Anyone who breathed in my space had to qualify for the use of the fucking air. Being on top was my only true satisfaction. Getting there, certainly, was more than half the fun, the whole ball game, at least until the point when I got older and saw some things differently. I guess I was seeking some degree of permanence in my life. Basically, I became more selective in the battles I chose to wage and, of course, win."

Sure, he readily admitted, he had "paid his dues." He had always been a bright, good-looking nobody who had "kissed the right asses" and "plowed a few prominent fields" to get ahead. "I made it a point to always be in the right spot at the right time with the right answers or at least a good bluff." Everything was always a game, and he made it all sound so easy for him. From all appearances, the course he had chosen had been easy—definitely rewarding.

The day's light had long been extinguished by the clouds on the drive to Savannah. It began to rain much harder as the couple approached the airport exit. When he increased the speed of the wipers, Marge again decided to risk provoking him by returning to the subject which had started the whole conversation. "I'm not sure how completely Wedge Reed fits into the picture as you've described it," she began and lit a cigarette. She was somewhat relieved that she managed to sound calm and almost detached.

"Hell, Marge, give me some credit," he snapped. "I know Wedge is no mental giant. Gerald Ford isn't the only politician who played football without wearing a helmet. But, goddammit, he's the ticket for what I want this time."

"What exactly do you want?" she repeated, reaching to open the ashtray, in hot pursuit of the opening he had provided.

"Okay, you're right. It *is* what *I* want. But not just me, understand? A lot of people are behind Wedge's campaign. I'm putting it together. I'm the prime mover in this thing, the one who will make it a reality. I always have. But there are plenty of others along for the damn ride."

"Oh, I'm sure they are, and I'm just as sure you will succeed."

"And why not?" he shot back. "Take a good look at the alternative in the party. Stew Harris is an asshole, a documented loaf of mental raisin bread. Only they even left out the raisins. This state wants more this time, and it sure as hell deserves better," he explained with no small degree of conviction. "North Carolina deserves more, and they're going to get it. Kent Reed will *be* the next governor. Not Stew Harris or some other upstart character."

"And you?" she asked, staring out the windshield. The rain was increasing steadily, but still Burns did not slow down.

"All right, Marge. What do you want me to say? That I'm in it *only* for myself? That I'm a greedy, scheming son of a bitch? Is that what you think? Would saying so make you happy?" With that, she knew she had succeeded. He was finally angry. But she wondered whether in succeeding she had actually failed at what she really wanted.

To avoid an immediate response, she reached and turned on the radio again. The music took up where the previous sounds had left off. To herself she admitted that she had gotten a definite reaction out of him. The first in several hours. But little else. And definitely not the reaction she wanted or needed, for that matter.

Later, as they drove closer to the airport terminal in silence, she extinguished the cigarette she had merely been holding for several minutes. She told him she had several offers to buy the condominium and would probably sell it at the end of the summer. She reminded him that she had originally agreed to buy the place with her sister, so that she and Burns would have a place for the two of them to meet away from Raleigh. Without pausing for a response from him, she said that she saw no reason to keep it, since it looked as if there would be less and less time for them to spend there. She saw no prospects of that changing from the sounds of the agenda he had outlined. She thought about adding "or less and less time to spend anywhere," but resisted making that final pronouncement. She honestly did not want to hear him confirm her fears any more than he already had.

The strains of an old movie theme on the radio provided an appropriate background for the increasingly bitter dose of reality and hurt she had acquired over the previous forty-eight hours. She settled back for the last few miles to the airport, letting the music play at will with her emotions. The striking presence of the rain merely added a dramatic reality to the chill she felt. The only words in the car were those of the weather report, which predicted even more rain. That was just another fact she felt needed no confirmation.

As on many previous happier occasions, she let him out at the curb at the departure area of the airport. He noticed at the time that she sped away faster than usual, but thought she was probably anxious to get back to Hilton Head before her sister arrived. Later, he recalled that she did seem upset. She hadn't offered her customary good-bye kiss, only drove away into the driving rain.

CHAPTER 6

The usual aggravation caused by the early morning traffic was lessened somewhat by the radio announcer's promise of a beautiful day for Raleigh following several days of spring rains. With the traffic moving faster than normal for an early Friday morning, Dr. Kenneth Harmon was on his way to his office after making his early rounds at Raleigh Memorial Hospital. Being a young plastic surgeon, he was particularly aware of the other automobiles, especially the lane jumpers and the accidents they caused. It was only his third day driving his new BMW 325e, the "toy," as his wife referred to it. It had been a gift to himself at the end of his first year in practice, a reward for years of doing without in a dark green, second-hand Pinto wagon.

He was only four blocks from his office, and for half an hour he actually appreciated the traffic delays which allowed him to linger in the soft leather comfort of the car a little longer. Charcoal gray and housing all the extras available, the BMW was a treat for the promising physician who had grown up in a small town near Charlotte, North Carolina, where his father had run an appliance fix-it shop.

The truth be known, Raleigh at any hour was a delight to Ken Harmon. He never regretted his decision to set up his medical practice in the city. And he was quick to assure anyone who asked that it had definitely been *his* decision. His wife, Caroline, was a Raleigh native and had intentionally said very little to influence him about the subject of where to locate his practice. For her, the thought of returning home was pleasing, much easier than, say, moving to Charleston, where her husband had received an offer from a prominent group of doctors to locate there. But the horror stories she had heard about Charleston and its entrenched social cliques had made her cringe. Nevertheless, she remained relatively silent on the subject and left the decision to her husband.

Ken Harmon left the small town of Overton near Charlotte at age eighteen. He entered the University of North Carolina where he met his future wife during their sophomore year. They had married after he completed the first year of medical school at Emory University in Atlanta. Both had worked hard while he was in medical school. His family could not help them financially, and they both preferred not to ask her parents for assistance. What they had, they achieved together. For the Harmons, a typical struggling medical student and wife, it was the best way, and neither regretted the lean years in bustling Atlanta.

Of course, Ken always realized how much his wife would probably love to live in Raleigh again. Both knew the city was big enough to allow them a life without too much interference from her prominent family. However, the real determining factor was his correct assessment of the other plastic surgeons practicing there. Those older, established types did not have the knowledge of the latest techniques, nor did they have Ken Harmon's personal touch with patients. Dr. Harmon had the know-how and the natural warmth that would work to his advantage in the medical community. So Raleigh was his choice.

Entering his office by the rear door, Ken Harmon could hear the computer keyboard chattering from the direction of the nurses' station adjacent to the reception area. He was hanging up his coat when Susan Graham came stalking down the hallway with a stack of files in her arms. A flaming redhead with a dimple in her left cheek, Susan had been a key factor in making the Harmon office, at least the part he shared in the suite with two older plastic surgeons, run as smoothly as it did.

"Susan, when did Mrs. Ward call?" he asked. He was holding a telephone message he found on his desk.

"Just a few minutes before you walked in," she replied. She laid down several files and handed him the ritual Styrofoam cup of coffee with the lid half open. "Mrs. Ward said to tell you she's found the *perfect* house and to call her as soon as possible this morning. Better do it now, too, before you leave for your meeting with Dr. Dunn and the committee at the clinic. Her number's on the note. She said she would be there in her office until about nine thirty, but not much longer after that and might be harder to reach later."

"Fine," he commented. Reaching for his white office coat, he instructed the nurse to pull a particular file for him. "I told Mrs. Galloway I would call her this morning, if the lab results were back. And, unless I miss my guess, that should be them in that top envelope."

"That's them. Her file is already under the envelope from the lab," she said, as she pulled them from the stack and handed both to him. "Do you need anything for the meeting? It's at ten o'clock in Dunn's private office at the hospital," she reminded him at the door, watching him cautiously maneuver the top from the coffee cup.

"No. I can't think of anything right now," he replied without looking up and without spilling a drop of the steaming coffee.

While scanning the lab report for Mrs. Galloway, he called and asked to speak to Jane Ward, who came on the line immediately. "Ken, good morning. I apologize for calling so early," the husky female voice rasped. "But your home phone was busy when I tried it. I think I have some good news for you and Caroline."

"Jane, we're beginning to panic. At least Caroline is. You can call any time you need to," he assured her. "Caroline probably had the telephone off the hook, so Kate could sleep as long as possible before she takes her to the daycare at the church," he explained. "What do you have this time?"

"Well, I know we've looked at a lot of homes over the past two months. But I've always felt you and Caroline weren't really excited about any of them," the realtor began. "But Ruth Brown

CUNNING Treatment

at Brown Realty was telling me last night that her agency is putting a house on the market today, and I believe we should look at it first. I drove past it on the way to the office this morning. I liked what I saw. Understand, I haven't been inside the house, but Ruth said it has four bedrooms, two full baths, and all the other things you are looking for. And it definitely is an old house, which you and Caroline seem to prefer. So many of the young people I work with do these days. And I can well understand when you consider the shoddy quality of some of the homes they're putting up today. Even the expensive ones."

"Jane, you know we'll look at anything you suggest. When can we see it?" he asked.

"Ruth told me she would not put up the sign or let anyone see it, if you could look at it before two o'clock this afternoon. I know it's short notice, but what's your schedule look like?" she inquired.

Glancing at his desk calendar, he said, "Early afternoon is clear. I'll make every effort to keep it that way. How about meeting me at the house at about one o'clock?"

"That's perfect. The house is at 4215 Valley Brook Road in Brookside. But don't let the address scare you. I know what price range you're looking for, and I think we can get it. I'll see you at one o'clock," she replied excitedly and immediately hung up before he could change his mind.

Ken Harmon finished his meeting with Dr. Dunn and the clinic committee at 12:30 sharp. Rather than return to his office for a sandwich the staff usually sent out for, he drove through the drive-through at McDonald's. It was exactly one o'clock when he turned onto Valley Brook Road and began looking for the 4200 block. Right after their daughter was born, he and his wife had thought about buying a bigger house. After six years of marriage, a series of apartments, one duplex, and a small house that neither had been particularly wild about, but could afford at the time, they had both wanted a home. "A real home with trees, high ceilings, and more than one bathroom," they both agreed.

Their search began with a call to Jane Ward, a friend of Caroline's parents, Wink and Ellen Collins. Jane had been selling real estate since the death of her husband, who had also been a doctor. Two months and at least twenty houses later, they had almost reconciled themselves to an overpriced house owned by a psychiatrist Ken did not care for professionally. As he turned onto Valley Brook Road, he turned off the Eagles tape and mentally crossed his fingers hoping that Jane had, indeed, found the right house.

* * *

"Burch, Cawthorn, and Holden," the voice answered. Ken reached Caroline at the architect firm where she worked three days a week as receptionist. "Until you get more established and I can pay for that English walnut chest I just bought" had been her reasoning.

Relieved she was the one who answered, he immediately told her about the call from Jane Ward and the house she had shown him. "Where is it?" she asked.

"It's on Valley Brook Road, close to your parents' friends, the Duggars, unless I'm wrong. If you can get away for a few minutes early this afternoon, Jane wants to meet us both back at the house. About four o'clock if that's okay with you. I gave her an earnest money check to hold until you can see the house. Why don't you call your mother and see if she can pick up Kate at the kindergarten? We can get her at your parents' house on the way home," he suggested. He knew how difficult it had been looking at the other houses with their daughter running around, disappearing into closets, and then crying because it was dark inside. He hoped to avoid that scene again if possible.

"That sounds fine to me, but I'll have to check with Mother and see how she feels today. You know how that is. Things are quiet here, since everyone's out of town at the new construction site in Charlotte. I can get Sue to cover the telephones for me. She won't mind. I'll be out front a little before four in case you're early," she said. "I'll just follow you to the house, and you won't have to bring me back to get my car."

"No, I'll pick you up. We can talk on the way to the house that way," he insisted.

The telephone rang at her desk. "Let me catch this other call. I'll see you at four."

CHAPTER 7

When they drove in the driveway at 4215 Valley Brook Road, Jane Ward's car was already there. Apparently she was waiting in the house or in the back yard. Ken and Caroline sat in his BMW waiting for Jane to appear. They looked at the house and then at each other. And smiled. They were a few minutes late, because they had ended up having to bring their daughter with them. After talking with her mother, Caroline realized it was best not to leave the child with her mother. "You know I would love to see her, Caroline. But I have this headache. I've just got to take something for it, and that always makes me so drowsy," Ellen Collins had explained. Caroline knew that what her mother took would undoubtedly be one hundred proof, and the amount would stagger a rogue elephant. So she and her husband had stopped by the kindergarten at the church to pick up their daughter.

Sitting in the car, Caroline spoke first. "Look at the size of that maple tree. And all those rose bushes!" Then they got out and stood by the car, waiting for Jane Ward to join them. Kate Harmon was squirming to get down from her mother's arms and wanted to run around.

"The garage roof looks like hell. But I can patch it myself for awhile," he said, referring to the dark brown wooden structure at the end of the drive and several feet from the house itself. "It might hold both cars, if those support beams are in good shape. I'll get it checked out before letting anyone near it."

"Sure. Just like that fence you put up and the plumbing you did where we are now," his wife teased. Each of those projects had been something less than successful. Ken had always helped his father in the appliance repair business when he was in high school. He continued to insist on doing many things around the house himself, despite Caroline's warnings and frequent reminders that they did not really save any money, since they usually had to call a professional repairman, whose job had only been increased by Ken's wanting to "do this one myself and save."

Their little girl was twenty-two months old. She fidgeted while her mother struggled to button her sweater. "Hi, Jane," Caroline said, as she handed the child to her husband with a sigh of relief.

"Ready to see one more?" the realtor asked enthusiastically and tweaked Kate's cheek, causing the child to squeal with delight. Kate had come to know and like "Mrs. Wad," as Kate called her, and knew Jane Ward always had a piece of gum or candy in her large purse. "I haven't seen the whole house, but I've told Ruth about you. She thinks it would be a good idea to let you see it first. And, oh, yes, be careful not to ask why the Campbells are selling. Ruth said Mr. Campbell does not want to sell, but is not stopping his wife, who definitely wants to. Ruth thinks they might be having marital problems."

"How long have they lived here?" Ken asked, as Jane again knocked on the front door.

"I think eighteen years or something like that. They have two grown daughters and one still at home. She's probably the one who will show us the house or at least let us in, I hope. I'll probably have to show it, and I can cover most everything. Ruth and I have discussed it thoroughly.

"Any questions I can't answer, I'll just have to get the answers from Ruth after we leave."

A girl of fifteen with long brown hair finally opened the door. "Hi, I'm Jane Ward, and these are the Harmons," she cheerily greeted the teenager. "We've come to see the house. I believe Ruth Brown called your mother this morning and said we would be coming over."

The house had an English cottage look, not quite Tudor, more rustic, and was only one level. Interspersed among the dark red, almost brown, brick exterior walls were randomly-placed gray field stones, which also had been used in framing the front walk. Hardwood floors throughout the house needed refinishing or "maybe just a good cleaning and some wax," Jane commented under her breath. Four bedrooms, a dining room, a large living room with functional wooden beams, and two beautiful field stone fireplaces, one in the living room and the other in the den downstairs, next to the basement. The huge kitchen with a separate eating area and the ten-foot ceilings throughout the house were particularly attractive to the Harmons. It appeared to be everything they had been looking for, since deciding to abandon their septic tank and other problems in their current house. The fact that the house only had two bathrooms bothered them, but Jane suggested they might check into having a half bath put in later, perhaps downstairs near the den. The realtor noticed their expressions when they entered the second bath which adjoined the master bedroom.

"Kids, this is an older house. You almost have to expect inevitable problems in the bathrooms, unless the owners have spent some money on them over the years. And it's probably a safe bet the Campbells have not. This is the size of every bathroom in any house you will see that's this vintage," she remarked candidly.

"Jane, how old is the house?" Ken asked, looking around to see if the Campbells' daughter was anywhere nearby.

"Well, to be exact, I'll have to check, but I believe Ruth said it was well over fifty years old, probably older. It was one of the first houses in this section of North Raleigh. The original owner owned all the property running up the hill back there and even had horses at one time, Ruth said. A small orchard, too, I think she said." The young Campbell daughter had rejoined them, but offered no comments. Apparently, the teenager did not want to leave the only house she had probably ever known.

CUNNING Treatment

A price tag of two hundred and sixty thousand dollars had been mentioned, which concerned both Harmons. He continued to look around the backyard where they had gone from the kitchen, trying not to look at his wife, who had just snapped at their daughter. He correctly guessed she might have done so out of frustration with the price of the house, which was obviously the one they wanted. "I know that's more than you had said you wanted to pay," Jane broke into their thoughts. "But it's definitely what I think you've been looking for all along. I hate to see you get less of a house than you really want and need."

"Do we have to let them know today?" he asked, still trying to pacify the squirming child.

"The 'For Sale' sign goes up as soon as I call Ruth. I promised to call her right after you leave here. You know I'm not trying to pressure you, but I just cannot ask Ruth to wait any longer. This house will sell quickly. You know that. You've seen what's on the market. Just look at this lot and where it is." Valley Brook Road was in a choice section of North Raleigh preferred by the up-and-coming crowd who revered brand names as if they were crown jewels.

A few minutes passed, more of looking at the house and quickly, at times, at each other, without either of the couple saying anything. Finally, Ken broke the silence. "You're right, Jane. The house is right for us. Tell Ruth Brown not to put up the sign. Dr. and Mrs. Harmon, one daughter, and one cat are moving in." He had made the decision. Caroline smiled and clutched his arm tightly. "Besides, I have to have this damn oak tree," he laughed, referring to the large, ancient oak that dominated the concrete patio in the back yard.

Within a few minutes, the Harmons and Jane Ward departed 4215 Valley Brook Road. Jane was asked to see that Ruth Brown got the papers prepared as soon as possible. The Harmons had at last found their "real" home.

✻ ✻ ✻

"How much longer are you going to keep that light on?" Caroline asked without turning over. They had gone to bed early, and their lovemaking had been purely mechanical and frustrating to her. They were both distracted by the decision to buy the Campbell house and all that decision meant for them.

"As soon as I finish this chapter, hopefully. But longer if that's what it takes for me to fall asleep. Do you want me to go into the den?" he offered half-heartedly. He knew the entire day had been difficult for her. First, the office, then her mother, and finally the decision about the house. And his own inability to concentrate long enough to give her the release she needed when they finally got into bed.

She did not reply to his weak offer to abandon the warmth of the bed, and go to the den which she knew might be cold after they turned back the heat. "Do you think we're doing the right thing about the house?" she asked bluntly.

"Sure." He was brief and positive. "We both like it, and it has great possibilities. Jane said we could always sell off part of the back of the property when we no longer want such a huge yard. We could probably get close to a hundred thousand dollars for it. And we'd still have the house and plenty of yard left."

Pulling back the sheet and blanket, she got up from the bed, walked to the bookcase, and turned on the small television. Lying back on her pillow, she said, "Well, sure, but that's a possibility down the road. Nearly three hundred thousand dollars is a lot of money for us right now. There will be a pretty stiff mortgage payment to go along with it, if my math's right. John and Glen are not paying you that well so far." She was referring to the older surgeons with whom her husband practiced. They had invited him to join their group, and the offer had originally seemed ideal. "At least they aren't now," she added without waiting for an answer.

Sitting up in bed, she pursued her thoughts with her arms wrapped around her up-drawn knees. "And it is an old house. I know we said we wanted one, but it seems to need a lot of work even now. We may find out it needs even more once we move in.

You know how expensive that can be. Just look at what we've had to fix around here, and this house is only twenty years old."

Placing the still-open book on his chest, her husband turned his gaze to her. "My turn. Okay?"

She relinquished and laid back down, staring at the late night television host who was delivering the usual boring monologue while still managing to draw guffaws from the tourists in his devoted audience.

"Yes, it is a lot of money. But real estate prices are going out of sight by the day. Pretty soon we couldn't buy half that house for that amount. And, yes, I know," he continued with some sarcasm slipping into his voice, "that my so-called colleagues seem to have the upper hand at the moment. But I'm not sure how much longer they will be able to maintain that hold."

Sitting up slowly and motioning with one hand while he held the book with the other, he elaborated. "Just like that asshole on the television, they're not what they used to be. Not by a long shot. My damn appointment load makes two of theirs. I'm young. I know the latest surgical methods, and, dammit, people do like me one helluva lot better than those two social snobs." Caroline turned on her side and looked at him as he spoke and began to unload. She knew the situation at the office was unpleasant and frustrating to him. But he rarely complained. She was even enjoying seeing him so animated.

He was still gesturing with his free hand. "Susan told me the other day how the office volume had increased. That's all *my* work. Those two dilettantes haven't had a new patient in months. Maybe years."

"Susan would say that," she teased. "She probably has a crush on you." She winked at her husband.

"Oh, sure. I'll just ignore that remark," he said. "And I know that house needs work. But there has to be some of it I can do myself. Hell, I may have to, at least until I can break away from John and Glen and go out on my own.

"But I'm convinced that house is right for us and Jane's right. It won't be on the market a minute once the sign goes up." He paused and grinned. "End of Harmon for the defense." With that, he slammed the book shut loudly, silently hoping the eyes staring at him across the bed would let the matter drop for the night.

With that dramatic gesture they both laughed and looked at each other. "I love you," she said and leaned over to kiss him. "We'll make it work. Don't worry," she said and they leaned back together. "Besides, you're going to be a rich and famous surgeon," she said, causing them both to snicker. They remembered how they had often fantasized while he was in medical school after their frequent hot dogs, macaroni and cheese, and too much wine.

"Yes, and that's that," he said. With the air cleared, he again picked up the Lawrence Sanders mystery he had been reading and said he was going to the den, but wouldn't be too long. "I've got early rounds at the hospital in the morning."

"Please turn off that fool," she requested, and turned her back to the television. "See you in the morning." Her husband did as she asked, as she turned off the light beside the bed. She again said, "I love you" as he disappeared down the hallway, careful not to make any noise that might wake their daughter as he passed her room.

CHAPTER 8

The charcoal gray BMW eased into the parking space marked "Plastic Surgery Associates #3." Ken Harmon got out and punched the automatic door lock. It was eight o'clock the morning following their decision to buy the Campbell house on Valley Brook Road. He had encountered no problems making his rounds at the hospital and was consequently at the office earlier than he expected. The only other car in the office spaces was the bright yellow Malibu with a license plate which simply read "SASSY."

"Hi, genius." The cheerful nurse in a white pants uniform greeted him as he passed through the outer office area. Only during peak office hours did he use the back entrance, for which he could rarely find his key.

"Good morning, Susan," he replied. "How's the coffee at this early hour? I don't think I've ever been here at this time of day."

"Well, it's just as well that you are here early today. You've got quite a string of 'em lined up," was the reply as she walked to the file cabinets across the room. "Do you know how many of these are yours?" She was running her fingers across the files that had been pulled for all three surgeons for the day. Without waiting for an answer, she elaborated. "You can tell by just looking at the new labels. Count 'em sometime. It ought to make you feel darn good, even if you are overworking us peons," Susan said, living up to her license plate. She was teasing, but had made her point. "This office was a piece of cake for us underlings until you came in and doubled the load almost overnight." They both laughed. She knew he appreciated the left-handed compliment.

Susan looked up and saw he was standing in the file room door grinning at her as she separated his files for the day's appointments. "I'm not complaining, understand," she said, enjoying the light banter which had become routine when she thought no one was listening.

"I know you're not, Susan. You're just afraid you'll break a nail opening all those file drawers," he remarked, still grinning.

"I'm really not. It just makes me furious, though, to see how well you are doing, to hear what your patients say about you, and then to hear those snobby SOB's we work for talk to you the way they do," she blurted. "It just isn't fair."

Still smiling, he turned to go to his private office down the hallway. "After you get those files together, I might like a cup of that coffee I smell whenever it's ready," he said. After she heard his door shut, she wondered out loud to herself, "How he can continue to work for those two bozos, I'll never know." The situation often made her angry. She vowed to never stop telling Ken Harmon how she felt about the subject. She had worked in several doctors' offices and realized how exceptional he was.

Ken Harmon had only been sitting in his office a short while when the office intercom on his desk announced, "Dr. Harmon, you have a call on line four. It's Mrs. Eric Matheson."

"Ask her if I can call her back," he replied. He was reading a particularly thick file for an early appointment and did not want to be interrupted. Within moments the receptionist's voice was back. "Mrs. Matheson wants an appointment for today if possible. I told her—" With that he picked up the receiver to take the call.

"Hi, Sally. How's my favorite tennis partner?" he asked, cherrily greeting Sally Matheson, who had been a friend of his and Caroline's for many years. Sally and Caroline had been Kappas in college and close friends in high school before that.

"I know you could kill me, Ken. But I really need to talk to you." His caller paused and then added, "I need to see you today, if possible." No matter what, Sally always had an urgency about whatever was on her mind. That urgency coupled with a tendency to scream and bitch a lot about everything had chased off husband number one. Now she was urgent about husband number two, a heavy drinker who needed anything but demands from his own second spouse, Sally.

"Just a minute," he said. He put her on hold and buzzed Susan. "Do I have any time available at all this afternoon?" he asked. He glanced at the large stack of files she had already pulled and thought his request would sound impossible, if not insane.

"Mrs. Thomas just called to cancel because her child is sick. She was scheduled in at two o'clock for a consultation" was the unexpected reply.

"That's fine. Put Sally Matheson down for that time," he instructed. "Thanks, Susan."

Returning to his caller, he asked how two o'clock would be for her. "Great, Ken. Just great," she said with some note of relief in her voice. "I was coming downtown anyway for lunch with my sister. I'll just stay longer and be at your office at two. But, Ken," she added with caution, "I must ask a favor. Please don't tell Eric I've called you. He would kill me. I will explain, I promise. You'll understand. See you at two." With that she hung up before he could respond to her request which, as usual, sounded overly dramatic.

He had already reached for the next file when he heard the click of the intercom and the receptionist announcing, "Mrs. Abbott is waiting in Room G."

Ken Harmon's private office was small and the last one down the hall from the main reception room. With the meager amount of money his paternal grandmother had left him the previous year, he and Caroline had carefully chosen a walnut English library table which he used for a desk, some second-hand hunt scenes which were in a grouping with his diplomas and licenses, and a brass lamp for the desk. The remainder of the money had been used along with some of his own money to buy an Oriental rug which he insisted on having. "I think the rug's colors will help give the room the warmth I think people need to feel when they see a doctor," he explained. The two chairs they had picked up at an estate yard sale Caroline had covered herself in a flame stitch fabric to match the rug. The predominant colors were dark blue and bittersweet, his favorites. There were, of course, several photographs of Caroline and Kate. There was also one taken of him as he finished the Atlanta Marathon, which he and some medical school classmates had entered on a dare from their wives during their last year at Emory.

A carved wood name plate that read "Dr. Kenneth Harmon" sat on the front of the desk. Beside it was an antique pen-and-ink stand that had been a gift from Caroline's parents, when he first set up his practice. The other items in the room included a trash can made from a large, spent ammunition shell he had found in high school on a field trip to an area where the army had held maneuvers during the Korean conflict.

* * *

As instructed, Susan showed Sally Matheson to Dr. Harmon's private office at precisely two o'clock. He had decided to see her there rather than in one of the regular examination rooms. "Well, that's one for the books," he remarked to Sally's back as he entered the room and closed the door before she could return around. She had been waiting in one of the flame stitch chairs in front of his desk.

Best described as Donna Mills having a really bad day, when her mousse had turned on her, Sally stood up, tossed her wavy auburn tresses, placed one arm around Ken Harmon's neck, and gave him a gentle, Junior League-variety buss on his left cheek. "You are so sweet to see me on such notice, Ken. And especially in here. I just love your little office," she began. "It's so personal. So like you," she gushed as he took his seat behind the desk.

"You damn well know all you have to do is call," he smiled, somewhat piqued at her "little" comment. "I've got to keep my tennis partner happy above all things. You've got me over a barrel and you know it." Pleased at the ease with which he flattered her, he continued. "Great dress, too." he added. "Get it on your trip last week? Somehow it reminds me of New Orleans."

"Yes, I did, Mr. Smarty. I made Eric buy it for me after the binge he and Bob went on one night. Helen and I were practically abandoned on Bourbon Street by those two," she explained. "We're still sick you and Caroline weren't able to go with us. Maybe next time. Have you found a house yet?"

"Believe it or not, after two months—two very long months and more houses than I ever care to see again—yesterday we bought a home. Not just a house. A home," he emphasized. "It's over on Valley Brook Road."

"Valley Brook! I love it! When can we see it?" she gushed, practically coming out of the chair. "Eric and I looked at a house over there a few years ago, right after we married, but it was too small and the basement looked like a dungeon. Do you mind if I smoke in here?" she asked, as she fished through a large tapestry handbag, not waiting for his reply.

"No, go ahead," he said and glanced over to make sure the room air cleaner was on. "We can't move in for awhile, but we're sure excited. You'll like the high ceilings, and you should see the yard! Kate can run wild. Flowers everywhere. And it's all fenced in in the back. Couldn't be more perfect for us. But lots of work for me, I predict."

"I can't wait to see it. But I know you are a busy, busy man, Ken darling, so let me tell you why I'm bothering you like this." A slow, drawling "darling" was Sally's trademark when she wanted something from someone.

"You're no bother, Sally," he assured her.

She went straight to the point. "I want a boob job or whatever you plastic surgeons call those things," she blurted without batting an eye. She immediately took a long drag on her cigarette.

Without looking toward her chest, he asked, "What brought this on?"

"It's not as sudden as you think," she said. "I thought about it when I was married to poor Jeff, but last week Eric's reaction to the tits and ass shows in New Orleans made up my mind. No problems with my butt, but these," she gestured with both her palms gripping the underside of her breasts, "are in need of improvement. Everyone's had it done but me. And your wife, of course. God, I wish I had Caroline's jugs."

Laughing at her comment about Caroline, he asked, "Are you asking my personal or professional opinion?"

"All right. I've already told Eric I was going to see Glen Parker about this, but I had rather see you first. You won't laugh at me. And Eric won't know the difference who I see," she clarified.

"I haven't ever thought anything was particularly wrong with the way you look," he stated. "And, besides, Sally, an augmentation is not to be taken lightly, despite what you may have heard around the pool at the club."

"Ken, surely you've noticed how flat I am," she protested. "You're just being nice to me, and I don't need that. At least not today. I'm serious about this."

"I can see you are."

"Well, will you help me or not?" she asked, putting him on the spot.

"Only to the point of recommending. I won't even consider performing surgery on my friends. You must know that. I wouldn't even sew up little Rick when he busted his lip," he reminded her. The Matheson's son, Rick, had bitten through his lower lip the previous summer when he fell off the slide at Mothers' Day Out at the Brookside Presbyterian Church.

"I understand that, Ken. What do you need to do to recommend?" she asked as she lit another of her Virginia Slims.

"First, I will make a preliminary examination. Then I will know more about what you might have in mind or actually need. Just a minute." He reached for the telephone and instructed the receptionist to hold his calls for the next few minutes. As he replaced the receiver, Sally Matheson was putting out her cigarette. "This is purely professional, you understand," he said. He leaned forward and placed his folded arms on the desk trying to look serious while maintaining a smile for Sally's benefit.

"Purely professional," she echoed seriously.

He then moved around the desk and standing beside her said, "All right, Mrs. Matheson, let's take a look."

She rose from the chair, placed her purse on the desk, and began unbuttoning her dress without really looking at him. He stood before her and looked at her breasts while she nervously held on to the back of the chair with one hand. He told her to stand up perfectly straight, as he gently touched and raised each breast. Carefully he pressed on both sides of each breast and told her to turn sideways for a profile. Without taking his hand off her left breast, he asked her to raise her left arm. As she responded, he pressed more firmly between the breast and the underarm area.

"When was the last time you had an examination?" he asked, while still pressing her left breast, only more firmly.

"Right after Rick was born," she replied. "About four years ago Dr. Bailey gave me a general examination when he put in my IUD. Why?"

"I can't tell right now. But it appears that you might have something here that needs checking before you think about an augmentation." She pulled away slightly. "Keep your arm up, Sally," he instructed, as she self-consciously began to lower it. "Have you noticed that before?" He took her right hand and placed it where he had been touching.

"No, I haven't," she replied hesitantly. "What do you think it might be?"

"I can't tell," he said. "And it may not be anything at all. But I recommend you let John McDonald see you. I'll make an appointment for you, if you want. I think you should just to be sure before you do anything else in that area."

He returned to his chair behind the desk as she slowly buttoned her dress. "This is a shitty note," she said.

She had finally managed to say something while fumbling in her purse again for her lighter. "Do you think it's serious?" she asked again.

CUNNING Treatment

"An augmentation would be relatively simple for you, Sally," he began, "but not until Dr. McDonald does anything he feels necessary about the other, if anything at all. That doesn't mean there's a problem, understand." He noticed her expression was blank.

He continued. "And don't get yourself upset over this. I can't have my tennis partner too distracted," he added to lighten the moment, aware of the mood swing that had come over her.

"Do you want me to see what John's schedule is while you're still here?" he offered again.

"Yes, go ahead, please," she finally responded. "But please don't tell Eric. Jesus, I'll tell him after I see Dr. McDonald. I promise."

While she sat there, Ken made the appointment. As she left the office considerably less self-confident than when she had arrived, he told her to call him after she had been to see McDonald the following day. Despite his reassurances, he saw that she was more upset than he would ever have expected Sally to be about anything. She had been through a lot in her life and had always come out a winner. He hoped her famous stamina would sustain her again, if McDonald diagnosed what he expected he would.

* * *

It was long past dark when Ken Harmon returned home. The full day at the office had been followed by a meeting with the hospital surgical staff and quick rounds to each patient on his roster.

He slowly entered the driveway and parked his car next to the aged green Pinto station wagon Caroline drove when it would start. Despite his initial protests, she had insisted on keeping it "for sentimental reasons." But he did have it repainted for her. As he stepped from his car he could smell the septic tank, which had plagued them for months. Good riddance he thought. "Good fucking riddance," he muttered to himself. Let the neighbors make their snide remarks to someone else from now on, he decided. He would never forgive the next door neighbors for calling the Health Department rather than saying something to him or Caroline first. When they did that, he vowed to move rather than give in to their tactics. He had had the septic tank repaired only to a degree sufficient to satisfy the Health Department. But he knew the neighbors would eventually insist on an entirely new tank and septic field. He would be damned if he would spend one more cent on that problem.

    Caroline was in the kitchen loading the dishwasher when he slid one arm around her waist and looked cautiously around the room. "Where's the little gremlin?" he asked in a whisper.

    "I put her to bed early. She fussed all afternoon. She still has a little trace of a cold. I gave her Tylenol and she dropped right off, thank God. She was exhausted. How was your day?"

    Before he could answer, she slipped from his grasp and moved toward the refrigerator. She opened it carefully and removed his dinner, which was neatly arranged on a plate and covered with aluminum foil. "Let me warm this for a minute. The oven's still hot. How about a glass of wine while you're waiting, sir?" she offered with some fanfare. "I've eaten, but I will join you for a drink if you don't mind cavorting with the hired help." She had gotten home much earlier than usual and was already in her most comfortable robe and thick socks from L. L. Bean.

    "Considering how elegantly you're dressed," he mused, "I had better accept your offer or you might crack me over the head with a skillet or something. I didn't know Ralph Cramden had a twin sister." With that he ducked down the hall just ahead of a ragged potholder Caroline tossed at him. He knew how much she loved that robe and those socks, but he never missed an opportunity to comment.

    When he returned to the kitchen, she was still trying to open the bottle of their favorite Chablis. "Thank God for this refrigerator and that stove. At least we won't have to buy new ones any time soon," she said. She reached for two wine glasses

CUNNING Treatment

from the cabinet and filled both. He quickly consumed half of his, reached for the bottle, and headed for the den. He turned and motioned quietly for her to follow.

As she joined him on the sofa in the den, the new house and all that had to be done was still on her mind. "But that clothes dryer is ready for the junk heap. Did you notice a clothesline at the house on Valley Brook?" she asked, and reached to place a coaster under the wine bottle on the table.

"No," he laughed. "But I think we can afford some really good wire for one. Do you think that will be all that acceptable in fashionable Brookside?" Both of them were constantly making light of the strict standards common to North Raleigh and to Brookside in particular. A favorite Sunday morning pastime was reading aloud the ridiculously sophomoric gossip column in the newspaper in which the obviously condescending writer tried her best to make Brookside society sound interesting or at best busy. Next they read selections from the *This Week On The Soaps* column, which to them had much more credence and the characters appeared less pretentious.

"I don't want to talk about money," she said sincerely. "I apologize for last night, and that's all I want to say about the subject. I'm much too tired and I'm sure you are too."

They took their glasses and leaned back on the plaid sofa her mother said they must have found at a yard sale in the wrong section of Raleigh. But a new sofa was not one of the Harmons' priorities, and so they continued to ignore her remarks. Ken removed his shoes and placed his feet on the stack of *Southern Living* magazines on the table.

"Jane Ward called today and said we could move in on the fifteenth of next month," she told him. Back to the house, he thought. It was a reflex action at this point.

"That would please the Andersons. Would you believe that bastard called again today? The minute I walked in the door. He asked if he and that creepy wife of his could move in here any sooner. That pushy bitch he's married to will get along just great with old Gloria next door. Those two will be quite a team or they just might kill each other. It can go either way with jerks like that. The rest of the neighbors deserve whatever happens."

He was glad to see his wife was in a more relaxed mood than the previous evening. "God," he laughed, "between Gloria and that damned septic tank, we sure will be getting rid of a lot of crap in one easy move." They both laughed, recalling the previous summer and their neighbor's crusade to clean up every septic tank on that side of Raleigh.

"I called Sally to see if she would keep Kate the day we move," she said. Caroline didn't want to have to ask her mother, if at all possible. "But she wasn't at home. Maybe I can catch her now," she said, reaching for the telephone beside the sofa.

Ken pulled her back and said, "You probably called her while she was in my office." With that news, he reached for the wine bottle and replenished both glasses.

"Your office?" she asked, surprised. Before he could answer she almost shouted. "I knew it! I just knew Sally would get around to having her boobs fixed sooner or later. She's talked about it ever since that clown in college offered her a football and told her to put it in her blouse during a Sig Ep keg party. Boy, did that sober her up. I knew it!" He was trying not to smile. "I'm right. I can tell by your expression. Well, are you going to do it for her?"

He was still trying to muffle his laughter, as he imagined Sally's expression when the charmer told her what to do with the football. Caroline continued with the questioning. "And I sure as hell bet she loved your examination. You did an examination, didn't you?"

"Yes. I examined our friend Sally briefly. And, no, I will not perform any surgery on her. You know how I feel about operating on friends. I referred her to John McDonald." He sipped some more from his wine glass, then dropped his bombshell. "Sally has a lump in her left breast. I told her to have John check it before she goes any further with anything."

Caroline leaned forward and slowly placed her glass on the table. Looking at her husband, she said, "Oh, damn!" There was some hint of guilt for her earlier remarks.

"Oh, damn," she repeated, now staring straight ahead.

"It's probably nothing, honey. John can take care of it as well as anyone, if anything does need to be done," he assured her, but felt somewhat curious about her reaction.

Then Caroline told him what he obviously did not know. "Sally's mother died of breast cancer," she stated.

"I didn't know that. We didn't get into her medical history," he said, then understanding his wife's reaction more clearly.

Each took another sip of wine. Suddenly, Caroline jumped up. "Your dinner," she cried. "It's probably ruined by now."

He pulled her back down on the sofa, only closer to him than before. "Screw the dinner," he said, nuzzling her neck. "Let's go to bed early."

She leaned down and kissed him on the forehead. "You smooth-talking devil," she said, and turned off the lamp.

He took the wine bottle with them as they walked arm in arm toward the bedroom, pausing only long enough in the kitchen to remove the plate from the oven. She was right. The slice of meatloaf closely resembled a hockey puck, the peas rabbit pellets.

CHAPTER 9

The Harmons' move to Valley Brook was not as difficult as they had anticipated. Luckily, nothing had been broken. The movers had patiently arranged and then rearranged the furniture to suit Caroline's changing preferences throughout the day. Her mother had ended up keeping Kate at the Collins's home, but had shown up sooner than expected, early in the afternoon. Once inside, Ellen Collins said she had to admit she approved of the house. She went into every nook and cranny and said she was "thrilled with everything" she saw. She was obviously equally thrilled with the idea of returning her grandchild earlier than originally agreed upon.

As expected, Ken Harmon had to be at Raleigh Memorial Hospital during most of the day of the move. Caroline reached him by telephone at his office right after the unexpected delivery by the men from the appliance store. "I love it! I love it ! I love it," she repeated into the telephone when her husband was finally on the line. "I never knew a clothes dryer could look so good or have so many dials. You are so sweet!"

As the movers were halfway through unloading the furniture, a truck had driven up and left a new clothes dryer, which Caroline directed them to put in the basement laundry area.

"Well, you deserve it. And besides," he added, "somehow I just can't picture a clothesline with ragged underwear flapping in the breeze on Valley Brook Road. I called the store just this morning after rounds. I can't believe they got to the house so fast. Must have been going that way anyway."

"I'm just glad they did. But when are they going to hook it up? They left before I realized the thing is still in the box downstairs. But I did peek inside."

"Have no fear, wife of mine. I'll have it running as soon as I get home, or at least by tomorrow," he promised. "The man at the appliance store said the instructions are very easy to follow. It's one of their newer models. I plan to be home most of the day after rounds, which will be nice for a change," he explained.

"Ken, why didn't you let the men who delivered the dryer just hook it up? They still could come back later, if they don't work on Saturdays," she begged. "It's probably a lot more complicated than you think, darling. I've looked in the box and something with all those dials couldn't be all that simple to install."

"Caroline, you don't install the dials, silly rabbit. That was done by the manufacturer. All that's left is probably a ground wire and the damn plug to the electricity. I can change out the plug, if it doesn't match the cord on the dryer. The dials have nothing to do with plugging in the dryer. And that's about all there is after the ground wire is connected. The dials will only be a problem when you have to operate it," he kidded her.

"At least get Eric to come over to help you," she continued her plea. She recalled his many other attempts around the house. Some had turned out somewhat less than successful, but she didn't want to offend him. After all, he had surprised her with the one appliance she most needed.

"Okay. I'll call him in the morning. But it's really not necessary. However, he can help me assemble that bookcase while he's there," he conceded. Before hanging up, he promised to be home as soon as possible that afternoon to help with the unpacking.

* * *

Having completed his rounds early the next morning, Dr. Kenneth Harmon was home by nine o'clock and would be, if he had his wish, for the rest of that Saturday, the one day he could catch up on whatever was left over from the previous week, which usually was quite a few things. There were still several boxes to unpack and, of course, the new clothes dryer remained in its container downstairs waiting to be installed. When he came through the kitchen, Caroline was dressing Kate after giving her a quick sponge bath in the sink. He told his wife he had not been able to reach Eric Matheson as promised, and asked whether she knew if the Mathesons had been going out of town.

"No, I don't think so. At least Sally hasn't said anything about that. That's why I suggested you call him. He's probably got an early tee time at the club," she suggested. "Why don't you call my father. He would love to come over. He hasn't been by yet, and he's probably waiting for one of us to invite him. He's not at all like so many others, including my mother, who barge in whenever they please."

"Now you know full well at nine o'clock on a beautiful Saturday morning—or even on a bad one for that matter—your father is on the golf course. Wink Collins doesn't miss a tee time," he laughed. "Look," he offered, "I'm going to hook up the clothes dryer myself. If for some reason I run into a problem, then I will call Heloise or someone for a helpful hint, if that's what it takes to make you happy." She was pleased and smiled to herself at his concession and watched him disappear down the basement steps. With Kate bathed and dressed, she had a long list of errands to accomplish and left with her daughter immediately.

Shortly before four o'clock that Saturday afternoon, Caroline and Kate returned home to Valley Brook Road. She was pleased to see her husband's car still in the driveway. That way, she thought, he would be available to entertain their daughter while she tried to master the dials on the new clothes dryer. One of her errands had been to pick up some liquid Tide and fabric softener. Entering the house she called Ken's name, but there was no reply. Probably asleep, she thought. She put Kate in her room to play and went to find him. Checking their bedroom, she saw he was not there. The bed was unoccupied except for the cat. In the kitchen she noticed that the basement door was lightly ajar, and the lights were on downstairs. She pulled the door open all the way. The empty dryer box sat at the foot of the steps. Again she called, but there was no response.

Proceeding down the basement steps, she still could not see beyond the stack of boxes that had been lined up along the wall by the movers. At the foot of the steps, she saw the dryer standing at a peculiar angle to the wall in the rear of the room next to the clothes washer. Her basket of dirty clothes had been placed on the top of the washer to get them out of the way. Behind the dryer she found her husband. The flashlight was still dimly burning. His right hand tightly gripped a screw driver. She later learned he had been dead for about an hour when she found him. There was nothing the paramedics could do.

CHAPTER 10

Carter Burns was pleased with the way many important things had gone over the previous several days. They had gone well for him and for the "Reed for Governor" organization. The attorney was satisfied that all the pieces were falling into place according to his design—and his iron will. He wanted the right people, his people, in the right niches, which meant under his thumb or at least another thumb he trusted. Finally, he had decided on an advertising/public relations firm to handle the Reed campaign. That decision had been crucial, carefully thought out for several weeks. There had been numerous meetings, as well as countless telephone calls to his office from agency heads who were confident they could "make the difference for Reed in this one."

Raleigh had been growing steadily for the previous twenty or so years. Insiders privately acknowledged that the city's growth was tightly controlled by the secret, all-powerful group that called itself Sequoyah. The group was made up of scions of the old money faction and their sons or sons-in-law, along with a handful of outsiders who at least went to Duke University and could be relied upon to follow the course set for Raleigh by the senior members. Sequoyah had no formal charter, bylaws or even a motto anyone ever knew about. The members were not bound together by words on paper, but rather by greed, self-interest, and a passion to control the city. They met at lunch in the exclusive Downtown Club in a private dining room above the First National Bank of Raleigh or occasionally at the Brookside Country Club. Never having an agenda, they got together whenever a member had something to discuss and usually went from there to discuss everything happening at that particular moment since their last meeting. They determined everything from whether anyone would make the right money from any given project to whether the membership at Brookside was getting too full of newcomers from out of town. Control had always been the watchword, and in Raleigh "Sequoyah" was the name of the game being played. Surprisingly, few people outside the group actually knew it existed. Most everyone knew the men who unofficially ran the city financially and socially, but few knew these same men were as organized as they were. If ever there was one, Sequoyah was an unholy alliance based on greed, good-old-boy backscratching, and a "we know what's best for Raleigh" ego shared by its members to a man. And rest assured they were all men. There had never been a female member of Sequoyah, and there never would be.

When Sequoyah began in the late 1950s, its power was infinite and unquestioned. However, in the late 1980s when the financial world had changed drastically with such innovations as interstate banking and outside money from New York and Dallas and even abroad, the group's grasp had been loosened somewhat. But not completely, by any stretch of the imagination. Carter Burns knew that all too well, and it suited his purposes. He knew he wanted the Sequoyah group's backing in the Reed campaign, but he was equally aware that under no circumstances could Reed be seen as their candidate. The Sequoyah support would have to be solid, but silent, at least as far as the public was concerned.

One way to accomplish that was to chose an advertising/public relations agency with connections to Sequoyah. There were two species of ties important in Raleigh: financial and family. The Edmundson Agency had both.

Not only did the Edmundson Agency include among its accounts the First National Bank of Raleigh and the Board of Trustees for Duke University; but Brenda Edmundson, the youngest daughter of Bert Edmundson, chairman of the agency, had married Todd Talmadge, Bryce T. Talmadge's youngest son. Burns knew the Edmundson Agency would have accounts such as the First National Bank and Duke, so long as Bryce Talmadge decreed it. Burns also knew Brenda Edmundson Talmadge would keep Todd for just as long as she wanted to put up with his well known drinking and the social missteps that only a Talamadge could get away with.

Despite some good smaller agencies in Raleigh and despite the temptation to use a top New York agency with an Atlanta office, Carter Burns did the prudent thing and elected to use a local firm. And the only real choice had been Edmundson. He felt it was right for Reed and would be right for Raleigh in the long run. And, of course, right for Burns, who prided himself in being able to see the "big picture" and the long range effect of each decision he made. He defined success as the result of solid preparation meeting golden opportunity. The fall election would be the opportunity, and the campaign and everyone connected with it would be well prepared. He would see to that personally. However, as in any campaign burdened by the post-Watergate rules of campaign financing, money would be a persistent concern demanding his constant attention. The money would have to be handled carefully, so as not to have Reed appear to be the creature of the PACs. Only certain PAC funds were acceptable to conservative North Carolinians. Yes, Burns had to acknowledge, he would have to "bird dog the finances from start to finish," as he put it.

The morning newspaper lay unopened on his desk. An abandoned cigarette was burning in the ashtray. Burns leaned back in his chair after asking his secretary to try and reach Judge Baxter before the judge left for court that morning. It was early, and the dark, cloudy sky made it seem even earlier than it was.

"Mr. Burns," the always pleasant and business-like Mary Cole spoke over the intercom, "I called Judge Baxter's office. He had not come in just yet. I left word that you needed to speak with him. I'll try again in about fifteen minutes if he hasn't called back by then."

"Fine, Mary," he responded, moving forward and pressing the brown lever on the intercom. "How about another cup of coffee when you have a chance?"

Sliding his chair slightly back, he opened the desk drawer. The envelope was still where he had placed it late the previous evening. He had stuck the long white envelope in the back of the cluttered drawer and marked it "Clippings." Burns gently pressed the envelope without removing it from the drawer to assure himself once more of its contents. Confident it was all there, he shut the drawer, reached for the newspaper, and placed it in front of him on the desk. The lead story concerned the first reports of a revolt in Saudi Arabia and the rumored role of the C.I.A. in the conflict between the ruling Saudi family and a radical element which opposed the official Saudi OPEC policy. That policy was causing considerable havoc in the western oil market, especially in the United States, where production had been curtailed for several years. To the top and left of the Saudi article was a smaller headline announcing that the city employees' insurance program had been awarded to the Hardwick Insurance Company in Raleigh. Burns reflected back to the envelope in the desk and its return address: Hardwick Insurance Company, Group Specialists, 812 West Parkway, Raleigh, North Carolina.

The door to his private office opened slowly as Mary Cole brought him a fresh cup of coffee. She had been with Burns for twelve years and was one of the few people he truly trusted and depended upon. She came over to the desk, sat the cup and saucer beside the newspaper, and placed his appointment list for the day on top of the paper. It was all part of the ritual to which they were both accustomed.

"Thank you, Mary," he said, as he picked up the list and leaned back to consider its contents.

"Will there be any changes you know of at this point?" she instinctively asked. "Do you still need to talk with Bob Franklin about the Turner case? I can try to reach him on his private number from here if you like," she offered.

"No. No changes I can see right now," he replied. "But don't make any additions without first asking me. And, if the mayor calls, put him through no matter what I'm doing. Don't use the intercom, if you need to let me know it's Reed and someone's in here. And you might call Doug Fessler's office and ask his secretary if he will call me about the motion in the Wilson case. Neither of us is ready for that one," he acknowledged. "But I think his client is pushing hard. Plaintiffs are like that. It's the nature of the beast—push, push, push—which is probably what got them in the mess they're in in the first place. Let me know if he wants to discuss the motion."

"Very well," she replied. As she moved away from the desk carrying a stack of papers she had removed from his out basket, she turned at the door and told him that Mr. Hardwick had left his overcoat the previous evening. She had placed it in her office closet.

"Send it over to Harkwick's office by the first law clerk who shows up this morning," he instructed.

"Will do," she replied. "John's usually the first one in. I'm sure he'll be glad to do it," she added and gently shut the door behind her.

A few minutes later the voice on the intercom told him that his wife was on line two. "Yes, Florence," he said into the receiver, after he first extinguished the remains of a cigarette and then again opened the newspaper to read while he talked.

"Carter, I meant to ask you this morning, but you got away before I could," she began.

"Meant to ask me what?" he asked.

"Are the Duggars coming to dinner tomorrow night or not? I've tried to reach Midge for two days and I keep missing her or the line's busy. She has one of those silly answering machines, but I refuse to talk to a machine. I suppose I could catch her at the club, but I hate to drive the car with the fender looking like that." Reminded of the situation with the car, she asked, "When are you going to get the car fixed? It's been three weeks at least since you had that law clerk take it in for an estimate."

"It's only been one week," he corrected her, as he quickly turned the newspaper page. "And, yes, the Duggars are coming tomorrow night. At least that's what Tom said before he and Bob Hardwick left my office last night."

"Oh, yes," she said, "I saw this morning's paper. How much did that cost Hardwick?"

"Anything else, Florence?" he asked, ignoring her last question and its obvious point. "Everyone will be at the house about eight o'clock. I need to go now. I promise to call about the car later today. Those parts should be in by now. Thanks for reminding me," he said in a more pleasant tone. "I'll see you about six tonight." With that they both hung up without saying "good-bye," which was their usual practice.

As soon as he hung up the receiver, Mary Cole entered with a third cup of coffee and told him Judge Baxter wanted him to call before nine o'clock if at all possible. "He called while you were talking to Mrs. Burns, and I didn't want to bother you," she explained. "Judge Baxter insisted I not interrupt you, but said he couldn't hold until you finished with your other call." Burns thanked her for the coffee and told her to get Judge Warren Baxter on his private line.

"Good morning, Judge," the always assertive Burns said rather loudly into the receiver. The judge's hearing was failing, and everyone spoke to him directly and louder than normal, particularly in the courtroom.

"Carter, I know you called me first, but I need to speak with you about something. So if you don't mind, I'll go first," the aging jurist began. "It's young Al Gregory. His father cornered me at lunch yesterday and reminded me that Al Jr. is getting out of law school next month. He's dead set on having me appoint the boy to my staff," he explained with some concern in his voice. "But I don't want to if I can avoid it. From what I've heard, young Al is just not up to the standards I've tried to set around here. You probably know that. I was wondering if I could refuse him without causing a problem in other areas."

Understanding the situation all too well, Burns addressed the problem with no hesitation. "Judge, we all know Al Jr. is not as sharp as his father and probably never will be. But you are right to ask, and I really appreciate it. This is a situation we should be careful with at this particular moment," Burns confirmed. The campaign was never far from his thoughts. "Al Sr. has been a lot of help to us in the past. You remember the housing fiasco," he reminded, as they both recalled the lawsuit, filed, but later withdrawn by a minority group, alleging discrimination in the allocation of federal grant funds by the City of Raleigh three years before. "You know as well as I do how messy that could have become if Al had not gotten that group to drop the suit. If they had persisted, God knows where that one would have ended up. That crowd in Washington was dying to get involved with that one. And it could have been murder for the mayor. Your denial of their class action status was crucial."

"I know, Carter. I know," the judge responded wearily. "But I've got some real talent here now, and they might resent the hell out of having Al Jr. thrown in with them. I know I would if I were in their places. They've all heard about how often he screwed up clerking at Ball, Weathersby and Sloan."

"I'll tell you what, Warren," Burns said. "Let me call Al and tell him I need his son in the campaign. That will kill time until he gets his law license. Hell, he may not even pass the bar exam. In the meantime, I will encourage his father to take him into his own firm where he can look after him. That's where he truly belongs. Let me talk to him. I'll get back to you later this week. I promise."

"Carter, thank you," the judge replied, relieved. "That will help me a great deal. I truly appreciate it. I really do."

"Don't give it another thought, Judge." The two men ended their conversation without Burns ever bringing up the matter about which he originally called. His political interests were far more important to Burns than any lawsuit.

CHAPTER 11

Al Gregory Sr. and Judge Baxter were not the only people Carter Burns concentrated on keeping in his camp. There was one Bryce T. Talmadge. And that took special efforts on Burns's part, given the nature of the man who was known around Raleigh as just "Bryce." Everyone knew what that name meant.

There were several aspects of Bryce T. Talmadge which might be described as exaggerated. His thick, curly eyebrows, his protruding stomach, which always made him seem to be falling slightly forward when he walked, and a large, somewhat rounded nose topping a puffy, effeminate mouth. There were also one or two other things which were not exaggerated in the least, the most discussed being his considerable wealth and power.

The Talmadge money had not, however, always belonged to Bryce Taylor Talmadge. He had overcome his own family's lack of means by marrying Artis Abernathy, daughter of Seth Abernathy II, founder of the Raleigh American Bank, Abernathy Real Estate, and Abernathy Paving and Construction, all located in Raleigh. Since the early 1900s, first Luke Abernathy, who drowned at age sixty-nine while duck hunting in Mississippi, and then his son Seth had amassed a fortune unrivaled in North Carolina and probably throughout the old Confederacy. By the time Bryce T. Talmadge went to work at Raleigh American Bank, the Abernathy money was, indeed, old money by most standards.

From the trust department at Raleigh American Bank, Bryce moved next to head the commercial loan department where he dutifully did Seth Abernathy's bidding on all matters of any significance. It was only a matter of time before Seth began

CUNNING Treatment

having young Talmadge out to the Abernathy mansion in Brookside for Saturday afternoon cocktails and poker and frequently a golf foursome at Brookside Country Club. When the marriage plans of Artis Elizabeth Abernathy to Bryce Taylor Talmadge were announced for June 3, 1949, in both Raleigh newspapers, many people privately wondered if Bryce had asked Artis or if Seth had asked Bryce to ask Artis or if Seth had told Artis to ask Bryce. Regardless, it was to be.

Following their elaborate nuptial ceremony and a three-week honeymoon trip to Europe, including a side excursion to Egypt and the pyramids at Giza, Artis and Bryce settled into the usual social patterns of Raleigh. Eventually, two sons were born to the couple, each of whom entered into various phases of the Abernathy family businesses, which had been taken over rather abruptly by his son-in-law when Seth Abernathy died in 1954 of a heart attack on the twelfth hole of Brookside Country Club. It was reported he made a dramatic chip shot out of a sand trap which went into the cup and sent the Abernathy scion into joyous, albeit fatal, leaps of ecstasy.

Being well-schooled in the ways of Raleigh society, especially the elite Abernathy variety, Bryce Talmadge set out to make it all his own. The name Abernathy remained on a building cornerstone or two, but by 1985, Bryce had made certain that everyone thought in terms of Talmadge money, not Abernathy. Large, well-reported gifts to Duke University, his alma mater. Generous, equally well-known gifts to charities, philanthropic foundations, scholarships, all in the name of Talmadge. Titles, civic awards, memberships on various national foundations for the arts and sciences, and, of course, membership in the all-powerful Sequoyah group. Everything was in the name of Bryce T. Talmadge, because he controlled the assets Seth Abernathy, a widower, had left his only child, Artis. And while his wealth and power could not be exaggerated, neither could his preference for young men.

Perhaps out of respect, perhaps out of genuine fear, perhaps out of both those things, no one in Raleigh ever spoke openly about what a halfway astute observer would see was Bryce's habit of always surrounding himself with attractive, bright young men. They were referred to around Raleigh as "Bryce's boys," but the implication was strictly fraternal in most people's minds. Some might even attribute it to his philanthropic nature. The older man saw a bright, struggling young man, more often than not a graduate from Duke University, and set him up in business with a good company, often a Talmadge company, and made sure the young man had plenty of business to justify his existence. What could be wrong with that? A young man and his family were fixed for life, so long as he paid Mr. Talmadge homage at Christmas, allowed a hug on special occasions, periodically joined Talmadge and his wife for dinner at Brookside Country Club, let Bryce buy him tickets for his private table at $1,000-per-plate political fund raisers, and participated in other little gestures to further his benefactor's interests. That was all that was required, unless someone were inclined to read between the lines and listened to his former daughters-in-law.

Both of Bryce Talmadges's sons were divorced by their wives, each having formidable financial means of their own prior to their marriages. Both times the secret divorce proceedings were held in the judge's private chambers, and all the records in the matter, particularly any discovery depositions, were ordered sealed, never to be open to the public.

Jean Burkes Talmadge had divorced Warren Talmadge, Bryce's oldest son, in 1980 for what the law in North Carolina euphemistically termed cruel and inhuman treatment. Few ever really wanted to know what that term meant. Her deposition, demanded by Bryce Talmadge just to see how much she knew and was willing to tell, was ordered sealed by the court following a call to the judge. The deposition revealed that she and her young son were afraid of the boy's father when he was drinking. But she had gone further. She elaborated in graphic detail about her husband's insistence on sitting on the patio in their fashionable Brookside home in his jockey shorts and eating pickles out of a jar. Those graphic food scenes were set out in the deposition in clear and unforgettable terms.

Her husband's attorney reluctantly pursued the pickle story with some delicate prodding. "Mrs. Talmadge, what was unusual about a man sitting on his own private patio eating pickles?"

The sharp-tongued Jean Talmadge was undeterred and more than willing to go on with the graphic details. She replied, "John, we've known each other for a long time. I sure as hell can't picture you sitting on your patio in your underwear eating anything, much less pickles."

"But what was wrong with pickles? Did he put peanut butter on them or something," the attorney prodded further.

"It wasn't peanut butter," she clarified.

"Well, what was it?"

"It was crap."

"What kind of crap?"

"Human. A more polite term would be feces."

"I don't understand."

"I wouldn't expect you to. As the saying goes, you had to be there."

The stunned attorney just sat there, not daring to look in the direction of his client, Warren Talmadge, who was staring out the office window and was being stared at by everyone else in the room.

Jean Talmadge did not wait for the next question. She finished the story on her own. "My husband frequently goes into the bathroom where he masturbates while sticking his finger up his butt. I've walked in on him more than once. He then goes to the kitchen to satisfy his other desires, which usually means he digs into the pickle jar while there is still crap under his nails. I've seen that, too. I only hope our little boy hasn't had the same experience of walking in on him. I did warn our son about the pickles. But I just told him those were his father's pickles, and he should never eat them." But she wasn't finished. "Once when he was drunk I actually asked him why he did that. I'm sure a lot of men masturbate. But I thought what Warren did had to be a little unique. He said his father had told him how." With that revelation, the deposition was abruptly ended by Warren Talmadge himself, who later instructed his attorney to negotiate a settlement as soon as possible.

Bryce's other former daughter-in-law told a similar story during her own divorce proceedings with the same results. However, Jean Talmadge's divorce requests went beyond a financial settlement. She insisted Bryce Talmadge was never to be alone with his grandson and demanded that be written in the divorce decree, which was also ordered sealed. Prior to the deposition, Bryce Talmadge had insisted the attorney for Abernathy Enterprises, Inc., be allowed to sit in on the divorce proceedings because of the "family financial" interests. That attorney was Carter Burns, who was pleased to have never been considered one of "Bryce's boys."

CHAPTER 12

Florence Burns and her husband had lived in Legend Hall for a little over five years. By the late 1970s the heirs of crusty Austin Cavanaugh had so squandered the family wealth that, as a last resort, they were forced to sell the old home place, which was known throughout eastern North Carolina as Legend Hall. Twice divorced, Niles Cavanaugh was the only family member still living in the antebellum mansion, and had contributed in his own way to the legend in recent years. Consequently, his two older sisters didn't hesitate to kick "Raleigh's Oldest Teenager" out of the house to which they had been invited less and less over the years.

Niles Cavanaugh was fifty-four at the time of the sale. A few years earlier he had begun dressing in drag in public, while playing around with his ever-changing band of "running buddies," who were always at least twenty years younger than he was. His favorite ensemble was a long wig as blonde as his own hair, a bright red chiffon dress, and red, size eleven "fuck me pumps," as he called them. Carter Burns was well aware of Niles's behavior. Serving as attorney for the Cavanaugh family, he jumped at the opportunity to buy their home place privately. "To help the family avoid the humiliation of a public sale," Burns said at the time.

The Legend Hall estate consisted of a two-story brick mansion built in 1858, surrounded on three sides with a verandah and gigantic white columns. Each column was topped by an ornate capital hand-carved from Tennessee limestone. The entire circular driveway was paved in brick to match the house and was lined with ancient, emerald boxwoods, some dating back to the original planting. There were the original servants' quarters and a hundred and seventy-five acres, mostly in pasture dotted with towering cedar trees. A dilapidated barn on the rear of the property had not been used in many years due to its condition.

Florence Burns particularly loved the home's spacious foyer. Made of black-and-white marble, its walls were the original murals of wooded European pastoral scenes. She insisted her husband also buy several valuable antique pieces and other furnishings from the Cavanaugh heirs, particularly the oriental rugs in the parlor and dining room. He liked the large pier mirror in the foyer, so it stayed, along with the eighteenth-century dining table which sat fourteen comfortably in Louis XV chairs with pettipoint cushions. All of the imported chandeliers remained with the house. In Florence's mind, and in the minds of many others in Raleigh, Legend Hall was second only to the Biltmore estate near Asheville, close to where her husband had grown up and where he had first realized there were finer things in life than being captain of the football team or selling life insurance to farmers. Invitations to Legend Hall were always eagerly accepted. Those summoned for dinner on the night of April 18 were no different.

"Come in. Come in," Carter shouted as he opened Legend Hall's graceful front door. It was seven-thirty. At their host's suggestion, Raleigh's mayor and his wife were the first to arrive for dinner. There was a minor, short-lived contest to see whether the Reeds or the Burns' golden retriever, Amberjack, would get through the door first.

"Wedge, I don't care if you are the mayor, you definitely do not, and I repeat, do not deserve this gal." He was referring to Charlotte Reed. She was the mayor's second wife, a former part-time model for a local department store. She and Kent Reed had married three summers earlier in a garden ceremony at Bryce Talmadge's home. Reed's first wife, Gayle, had taken her own life following the leukemia death of their only son at age fifteen.

The first time Burns had ever met—or at least almost met—Charlotte Sanders she was having sex with the mayor on the leather sofa in Byron Holt's office. Holt was a close friend of Burns's and editor of the Raleigh morning newspaper. The attorney had walked into Holt's private office expecting to see the editor on business. Instead, he was confronted by the imposing edifice of Charlotte's bare buttocks riding the mayor like a professional broncobuster at the Oklahoma State Fair. Her back was to the door. Reed only momentarily glanced from under Charlotte's right arm, as Burns carefully closed the door and left. Two years later when Reed's wife committed suicide, the mayor and Charlotte were married, and Burns served as best man. Neither he nor Reed had ever referred to the episode in the newspaper editor's office.

Burns still had Charlotte Reed in his grasp at the door when his wife, Florence, entered the foyer, wiping her hands on a dish towel. Always bouncy, Florence was beginning to look slightly older than her husband and her fifty-six years. But she knew how to take command of a situation on her own turf. Legend Hall was controlled by its mistress. She gladly left the rest of the world to her husband.

"All right, Wedge," Florence laughed, "you just come with me and help for just one minute in the kitchen while these two get untangled." Taking the mayor by his elbow, she led him down the hallway, just as the noise of other arrivals filled the elegant entrance hall.

Midge and Bryce Talmadge arrived last. They were preceded by the Craigs, the Taylors, and the Andersons. Charles Craig, president of the First National Bank of Raleigh, and his wife Bess. Dr. John Taylor, a dentist and current president of the prestigious Brookside Country Club, and his wife Joan. And Avery Anderson, a wealthy building contractor, and his new wife Vivian. The men comprised the mayor's biggest and most loyal financial backers. Each was important to the upcoming and all-important gubernatorial race. Individually, they had encouraged Reed's past ambitions for their own reasons. Each had a personal stake in his continued success at the polls, but none more than his long-time friend, the evening's gracious host.

CUNNING Treatment

Throughout his political career, "Wedge" Reed had expertly run the "plays," as he called them. But the plays always originated on the sidelines with his coach, Carter Burns. The team was guided by the self-interests of the manipulators who cheered each successful run loudly. They had the money to make it all happen for Kent Reed. He was the ticket, the whole show. Being good at what he did, Reed pleased his backers, and they profited accordingly. The stage being set for the next big contest was being previewed that April evening during the select gathering at Legend Hall.

The large, silk-walled dining room overlooked the garden of the Burns mansion. The garden was immaculately appointed, and the perennials were just beginning to emerge. Carefully placed candles in hurricane lamps gave the garden a wistful, warm glow. Inside, a large floral arrangement of yellow spider mums, purple miniature iris, fern stems, and a touch of fuchsia, from the Bucket Shoppe, graced the center of the huge table, which was also lit by four silver candelabras. Each lady's plate held a single yellow rose, a special touch of the hostess, who took great pleasure in all the details for such an occasion, to the delight of her husband, who loved to bask in his wife's success.

Not a champion of women's liberation, but also not a female step-and-fetch-it for anyone, including her husband, Florence knew exactly what she stood for and wanted in life. And she expressed it with class. "I admire Gloria Steinem and all that," she admitted, "but I don't feel any need to burn my stove mitt for anything other than a good rack of lamb." She refused to color the touch of gray in her hair and preferred a soft, feminine look in her clothes. Silk print dresses, tailored suits, and cavernous purses "to hold everything I need," and, above all, comfortable shoes. She had a standing weekly appointment to have her soft, simply cut, dark brown hair done, but insisted on doing her own nails which she said relaxed her. Twice a year, she flew with a friend to New York for a week of shopping, although she usually spent more time in museums than in Bloomingdale's or Bergdorf's, and she preferred Saks "because the clerks always seem more friendly."

A collector of cookbooks, Florence took particular pride in planning a menu, especially enjoying the reaction of her guests to each course. The praise from her husband was also important to her. That April evening for the Reeds' dinner, the first course was a light cream of asparagus soup with a small serving of homemade croutons, lightly seasoned with parsley and garlic. Next a spinach salad with thin sliced hard-boiled eggs and a warm bacon-and-olive-oil dressing she had begged the recipe for from the chef of her favorite Italian restaurant in Atlanta. For the main course, she pulled out the last of the quail from the freezer and prepared it as only another Florence—Dufresne—recommended in one of her favorite game cookbooks. The quail were accompanied by tiny glazed carrots in a light lemon sauce, small boiled potatoes, and exquisite little rolls from Raleigh's "only true French bakery," La Baguette. Dessert was homemade vanilla ice cream topped with raspberries accompanied by crisp English butter cookies. After any dinner, the coffee and liqueurs were always her husband's contribution to the fine meal.

To assist her with the house Florence had a maid five days a week. There were also two female college students who were asked to run errands and to help on special occasions. In exchange for helping, the young women lived free in the renovated servants' quarters across the garden from the main house. The students often provided company for Florence when her husband was away on business, and they always appreciated the Burns "scholarship," as it was called on the nearby university campus.

"I talked with Greg Barlow," Burns said to Kent Reed, who was seated as always on the host's right. "I feel certain he can be a big help to us in many ways. At first he didn't think he would have the time to be campaign treasurer, but I believe he'll come around. Frankly, he can't afford to say 'no.' Not when you consider the opportunities with this particular campaign. Now, John—"

Florence broke in from the other end of the table. "Wait a minute, Carter." All heads turned to their hostess. "You men can scheme all day long and all night, as I'm sure you do," she laughed, "but I want to hear what Charlotte thinks about all these plans. Being the wife of the mayor of Raleigh is one thing. Being the wife of the governor of the entire state of North Carolina is quite another." Enjoying her audience, she continued. "It's one thing to campaign in this city, but the whole state is a lot of ground to cover."

With that, the attention of everyone at the table immediately shifted to Charlotte Reed, who sat midway down the table next to a grinning Bryce Talmadge, who hastily whispered something to Charlotte which she did not hear. She surveyed the expressions of the other guests before stopping at her husband's. "I think the campaign sounds very exciting. Whatever Wedge wants me to do, I'll just do it."

Charlotte Reed's endorsement of her husband's plans sounded a little tepid to her hostess, who said nothing. That response was almost pat and a little too gushy for a realist such as Florence.

"I'm just going along for the ride," Charlotte added, smiling at her husband. Burns was immediately reminded of her backside on her earlier ride in the newspaper editor's office. She was without a doubt up to it, he thought to himself.

But Florence could wait no longer. "Oh, hogwash, Charlotte," she blurted out. "That will sound just fine in the newspapers, but you must know what a price a politician's wife pays." With that remark several of the guests around the table thought back to Gayle Reed and how she had quietly tolerated the pressures of life in politics, not to mention Kent Reed's philandering. Florence had long suspected that the evening's guest of honor had shared a relationship with the lovely Charlotte long before his wife's suicide. She even wondered if that relationship had somehow played a role in Gayle Reed's tragic death.

"Florence, you heard Charlotte," Carter broke in. "She's accustomed to the public eye. And not all that bad for it," he laughed. Everyone welcomed the break in the moment's tension. "Wedge knows what he wants and he's going to have it. They both want it," he emphasized and winked at Charlotte, who was grateful for the change of tone in the conversation.

"Well, it's not just what he wants," Charles Craig broke in with some force. "A lot of people in the Democratic Party want to offer North Carolina an alternative to that political bumpkin Stewart Harris. Hell, his father, when he was governor, turned the state over to his sister Louise. Probably a good thing he did. During his last term, he was out of the state most of the time. And old Stew will just give it right back to that overbearing bitch, if he's elected. Harris is too stupid to understand how to run a golf cart, much less North Carolina." Stewart Harris's lack of intelligence was a matter of record in some circles. "You know it's pretty damn difficult to flunk out of the state university when your father's governor and head of the Board of Trustees. But good old Stew managed that one all on his own. He didn't need Aunt Louise to accomplish that little feat."

"You've hit that particular nail solidly on the head, Charlie." Burns had to get his opinion in. "But aside from that aspect of it all, Wedge is simply the best candidate around. That's why we're here tonight. All of North Carolina is ready for a step forward. Ready for a change. A big one. And Wedge is going to give it to them."

"We almost got an unwanted change of things recently," Avery Anderson offered in a definitely serious tone. "Kip Fowler almost ended his career permanently in that damn plane accident." He reminded the others sitting at the table about the near fatal crash and subsequent emergency surgery for their state's junior United States Senator.

"I heard that Lenore Fowler couldn't get back in time for the surgery," Florence added. "She was on a cruise through the Alaskan fjords and was actually with a group of people on a glacier. She didn't even know about Kip until she got back to the ship that night. I think a special helicopter had to take her off the ship to a port where she had to fly to Anchorage before catching a commercial flight to Seattle and finally back to Raleigh."

CUNNING Treatment

"Well, if anyone can scramble in a difficult situation, Lenore can. She's called her share of the shots in that family for a long, long time. Where was Jonathan Sr. when the accident happened? Was he with Lenore on the cruise?" Carter asked. He was aware of the accident, but none of the particulars, being preoccupied with other, more important things.

"No," Charlie Craig continued the story. "Jonathan was here and went straight to the hospital where Kip was taken." Then recalling how former United States Senator Jonathan Fowler and his only son had never been known to be close when Kip was growing up, Craig remarked, "It's good to see the Fowlers together more now. I guess now that Kip's in the Senate himself, they have more in common or something. Jonathan always was a snob. A royal pain. Thank God Kip's nothing like him. But they do seem to be closer now. Maybe the forced retirement mellowed the old man."

"It probably hasn't slowed down Lenore," Bess Craig chimed in. Everyone at the table knew exactly what she meant. "She's always been the brain behind all the Fowlers. If anyone ever asked her husband a question, you could bet Lenore either answered or told him what to say. It all came from Lenore, one way or the other."

"You must admit, though, Kip has a marvelous future." This was from Florence's end of the table. "Why every time you turn on the television news, even on those talk shows, there's his handsome face discussing something vital to the country. He must be on every important committee in Washington."

Charlie Craig had more to say on the subject. "Whatever Kip's got, he sure as hell didn't get it from Jonathan. That man was a pontificating, one-note ass. That did him in as much as anything else. Kip's got what it takes, but his old man can't take credit. That's for damn sure."

Burns just sat there pensively listening to every word. He thought to himself, "Charlie, you don't know how very right you are. So very, very right."

Kent Reed asked if the Fowlers were going to back Stewart Harris, whether he ran as a Democrat or not. Burns quickly spoke up. "Well, I haven't heard either way from any of their people. I do plan to see the Fowlers, particularly Lenore. I want to ask her that very question at the right moment. There's no need to rush into that one right now. There's time."

Wanting to move the focus away from controversy, Florence decided the evening had been dominated by politics long enough, even though she did enjoy hearing everyone's take on such matters. "We're also here to enjoy some good company," she interjected. "Joan, how did your doubles match come out today at the club?" she asked. The others took her cue and settled into smaller conversations.

After asking with a certain amount of flair who wanted coffee or brandy or a liqueur, the evening's host began serving each guest according to their wishes. Bryce Talmadge wanted both coffee and brandy, causing his host to mentally acknowledge that at least his guest was consistent, even when it came to after-dinner drinks.

Florence was receiving her coffee last, when one of the students helping in the kitchen entered the dining room and quietly told her Ellen Collins was on the telephone and seemed quite upset. Florence thanked the young woman and excused herself. She went into the study and took the call there. She was gone longer than expected and was visibly shaken when she returned to her guests.

Taking her seat, she began. "I'm afraid I have some terrible news. That call was from Ellen Collins. Her son-in-law was killed this afternoon. You all know Dr. Kenneth Harmon. He married Caroline Collins." She paused to drink some water. "I'm not really sure what happened. Ellen is in quite bad shape, as you might expect. I think she said he was electrocuted by something. At least, that's what I think I understood her to say. I'm not sure Ellen actually knows herself. This is so terrible. I just can't imagine." Her voice trailed off as she again reached for her water goblet.

After a few more moments of conversation, and seeing how upset their hostess was, the evening's guests excused themselves. Burns saw each of them to the door and returned to the study where Florence had retreated. "Do you think we ought to go over to Wink and Ellen's?" he asked, taking a place next to her on the sofa.

"No, not tonight, please. In the morning will be soon enough," she softly insisted. "Caroline and her little girl are staying with Wink and Ellen tonight. They'll be all right. I had rather avoid the initial emotional shock in that house. Ken meant so much to that family. No, tomorrow will be better. We can go early as you want. I just think I need to stay here tonight."

He asked her to repeat what Ellen Collins had told her. "Oh, darling, I'm not sure. I'm really not. We'll just have to find out the details tomorrow morning. Ellen was so upset. And she had had too much to drink. I am sure of that. I do remember her saying they found him in the basement of their new home. It's on Valley Brook Road. Ellen and Caroline had been out shopping. Caroline just found him when she returned. I can't imagine. I just can't."

CHAPTER 13

The next morning arrived much sooner than Florence wished. The car radio announced the ten o'clock weather forecast just as her husband drove them into the Collins' driveway. Ten o'clock had been as long as she could stall him. She knew at least he was anxious to pay their respects to their long-time friends. In the past the Burns and Collins families had been closer than they were. Each family had a daughter the same age, and the two families had enjoyed many good times while the girls grew up. They had shared dinner tables at Brookside Country Club on many occasions. Their daughters had been inseparable, until Jenny Burns was killed in an automobile accident by a drunk driver.

As they drove up the Collins' driveway toward the Georgian home, Carter recognized John Arthur's green Jaguar and Ben Hastings's black BMW parked in the drive. "Carter," Florence said as he opened her car door, "please, let's not stay too awfully long. You know how I hate things like this. Tell Wink something at the office is urgent and come and get me, if I'm alone with Ellen too long. I'll tell her I might come back later." But she knew that would not be anything she intended to do.

"Maybe she would like to come over to our house later. Just to get away. I suppose it all depends on how Caroline is doing. We'll just have to see," she continued, as though she was thinking out loud. She desperately wanted a strategy to use to rescue herself from the emotional scene she knew was waiting inside the Collins' home. Nervously, she gathered her black cashmere coat tightly around her, as they started up the front steps together.

They were greeted by the maid who took their coats. She told them Caroline was in the Collins study with her daughter. Florence used that as an excuse to avoid confronting Ellen Collins a little longer. She simply said "Caroline" as she placed her left arm around Ken Harmon's widow who quickly rose from a chair to greet her parents' long-time friends. Caroline's daughter, Kate, was playing with a large wooden puzzle on the floor near the center of the room. The two women then sat without speaking for a moment. Because of a late spring chill, there was a fire in the fireplace, which needed stoking. Caroline reached for a poker and moved to set aside the fire screen.

With her back to Florence Burns, she began to discuss what had transpired. "You know, Mrs. Burns, it really isn't fair. You know, right now I'm actually more angry than sad. Ken had worked so damn hard. So hard. He genuinely cared so much for people. He worked so hard on so many things and expected so little in return."

Sitting back down beside Florence, she reached to take a piece of paper away from her daughter. "I'm sorry. I didn't mean to sound so resentful. But I guess I am. Crying is the last thing I need to do after last night," she confessed. She had refused her doctor's offer of a mild sedative to help her sleep, instead spending the night alone in her old bedroom upstairs. Too young to understand, Kate had gone to bed early in the room next to her mother's.

"Caroline," Florence began, "I can't totally recall what your mother said when she called last evening. I was in such a state of shock. How did it happen?"

The young woman then began to recount what she had been going over and over for hours. "Ken was down in the basement. He was hooking up a new clothes dryer, which he assured me was simple enough to do. He was always doing little things like that wherever we lived. He had just bought the dryer for me as a surprise when we moved, and he was . . ." She paused to take the fire poker away from her daughter.

"He was installing it in the basement. Kate and I were out shopping with Mother. She had come by to take us to lunch and that new children's shop in the mall. When we got back, mother went on home. I just went downstairs and there he was. He was still holding the damn screwdriver in his hand." She looked toward the fire with angry tears in her eyes. "A damn clothes dryer. A stupid, goddamned clothes dryer. What could have gone wrong?" she wondered out loud.

At that moment Burns entered the room. He had left Wink Collins in the kitchen where he was making more coffee for the others who were still in the living room. Carter placed his hand on Caroline's shoulder, giving it a squeeze. "Florence, Ellen's upstairs. Why don't you go up and speak with her? I want to visit with Caroline for a moment before we have to go."

As Florence stood to leave the room and do as he suggested, Caroline thanked him. "I'm okay. You go on and be with Daddy, Mr. Burns. I need to keep an eye on Kate. I'll be all right alone."

Catching his wife at the bottom of the staircase, he warned her. "Just keep your thoughts together. I know this will bring back a lot of painful memories. It does for me, too. But we have to. Wink and Ellen would do it for us. We won't stay much longer. I promise."

The door to Ellen Collins's bedroom was partially open. Florence could see her even before she entered the room. She could see Ellen, poor Ellen, as she frequently thought of her, reclining on the chaise lounge on the other side of the room where she had probably been for hours. She was staring out the large bay window. Florence saw that she was dressed and had undoubtedly never gone to bed the night before. She appeared more to be clutching her blue cardigan around her than just wearing it.

Her visitor was already in the room standing beside her before Ellen slowly looked up. Her eyes were practically black from crying. Her face had little other color, only adding to the painful drama of her eyes. It had been a night of anguish and grief, and, as Florence knew, much self-pity. With hesitation, Florence grasped her friend's left hand as she sat down beside her, wanting to speak, but unable to find the strength to say anything.

Eventually, the grieving woman looked up at Florence, only to resume staring out the window at the fields behind the house just beyond the pool which still wore its winter cover. Finally, the silence was broken. "Oh, Florence, he was so fine. So damned decent. God, he had such a career ahead of him. Everyone knew that." She paused, then went on with her thoughts. "Wink and I loved him so." Florence wanted to say something, but still no words were there.

"Ken and Caroline had worked so hard together." As if to clarify, she said, "It was his idea to set up his practice here. Caroline would have gone anywhere he wanted. Anywhere. He knew that. Caroline's a real trooper. One of the best. There wasn't anything she and your sweet Jenny couldn't accomplish growing up."

Florence looked out the window at the same fields where her daughter and Caroline Collins had ridden horses, played softball, and done a million other things for as long as they had known each other. Those memories only deepened her silence.

When she had first entered Ellen's bedroom, Florence had noticed the almost empty glass sitting on a small table beside the lounge. It was not yet even eleven o'clock in the morning, but she knew Ellen had already been drinking her essential bourbon, probably throughout the night. And she understood. God, I understand all too well, she admitted to herself. When Jenny died . . . She stopped her thoughts there. She would not allow them to go further.

Finally, Florence spoke. "Ellen, Carter and I . . ." But that was a far as she got.

"Oh, damn, Florence. It's all so rotten. What did we do to deserve this?" It was a demand as much as a question. "Ken meant so much to this family. Especially after all we've been through." At that point her tone took a deep roller coaster slide from sorrow to caustic bitterness.

"Particularly after all the crap. Florence, how have Wink and I gotten through the past two years? Sometimes I do not honestly know. It's been one living hell. You, of all people, must know that. I don't have to tell you what we've had to endure. One horrible thing after another. And now . . . this." Florence braced herself for the onslaught she had longed so desperately to avoid. But to no avail.

"When I think about what we have been put through in this town. All the stories. The lies. All the cheap shots from people we thought were our friends." She reached for the now empty glass, stood up, and walked to the bookcase where she found the bottle of Jack Daniel's among the bric-a-brac. From across the room, she resumed recounting the details of her ordeal. "Sure, I've heard the whispers and giggles at the club that suddenly break off when I get too close. Arden Simpkins Moore didn't know I was in the ladies' locker room the other day, when she was entertaining a few of the newer members with the latest dirt on old Wink and Ellen Collins. Why, apparently, her audience doesn't know Miss Arden from her days as a roaming divorcee slash cocktail waitress in Atlanta." She paused, then added with biting emphasis, "Waitress and whore. That was before the bitch broke up Ralph Moore's marriage and claimed that simpleton and all his money for herself. Now she's Miss Goodie Two-Shoes. Oh, it was quite a show she was putting on for her fancy new friends. I can assure you of that. Most of them are as simple-minded as she is."

Wanting somehow to escape, Florence sat frozen in her own private grief. She watched as Ellen moved slowly to the window where she stood addressing the outside, as if there were an audience. But there was only an audience of one. Suddenly, Florence feared Carter had forgotten his promise to leave.

"And, yes, my friend. We've taken much more than our fair share. Well, I say fuck it all." Ellen took a quick swallow of the bourbon. "You know what, Florence. People our age don't say 'fuck' nearly enough. We seem to think it's the younger generation's word or something. I don't know. Well, I say 'fuck' a lot. Fuck. Fuck Arden Moore. Fuck Wink's thieving ex-partners. And fuck—"

The bedroom door opened slowly. Carter had heard the last of Ellen's bitter, drunken soliloquy. He motioned for Florence to just follow him. She muttered to Ellen that she had to go but might return later. As she left, Ellen was pouring another glass of bourbon. She never saw Carter, who thought it was better to leave her alone than try and console her at that particular moment. He knew there would be ample occasions over the days to follow.

During the drive back to Legend Hall, Florence told him about her fears and the gnawing memories of their Jenny's death. "Just keep your mind off the Collinses," he advised. "There's nothing you can do now. They'll get through it." He reached for her hand on the seat beside him and held it.

"I want to put fresh flowers on Jenny's grave before Ken Harmon's funeral," she remarked as she gazed out the car window.

"I'll tell Mary to order them tomorrow."

"No, I want to do it myself." She was afraid he might get busy with the Reed campaign and forget. She knew all too well that her husband's priorities often were not the same as hers.

CHAPTER 14

Florence Burns was standing beside her husband. They were in their driveway looking at her car. A mechanic from the repair shop had just delivered her Seville after restoring the car's right front fender. She remarked that she had never expected to see the car look that good again. The anxious young mechanic apologized for taking so long to do the work and appeared relieved when his ride back to the repair shop finally arrived. Carter Burns frequently had that effect on some people.

As they entered the house, she told her husband that she had spent the afternoon with Ellen Collins playing bridge in a private room at Brookside. It was several days after Ken Harmon's funeral, and Florence had insisted Ellen get out of the house. "By the way, Carter, I told Ellen you would speak with Caroline when she's ready to talk about some matters. Ken's will and all that sort of thing," she explained. "I hope you don't mind. Ellen and Wink feel so helpless. It's no secret they can't help her as much as they would like to or could have a few years ago. They're both drained, emotionally and financially. Please call her when you can. Caroline, not Ellen," she clarified. "It would mean so much to all of them. To know they have someone they can call on. I'm afraid I haven't been much help to anyone in this," she added regretfully. They both knew what she meant. He placed his arm around her shoulders and promised he would be available whenever Caroline wanted.

"In fact, I will call her. No harm in that," Burns offered. "Maybe I can be of some assistance. She will probably need encouragement to get on with things as soon as possible. Caroline's a fine girl. But it's easy to let such matters slide for a

CUNNING Treatment

while. She needs to get them all behind her as much as she can. The sooner the better. I'll call and suggest she make an appointment. I'd prefer see her at the office, rather than her home or ours. And certainly not at Wink and Ellen's"

When Ken Harmon's name came up in a conversation at the office a few days later, Burns was reminded of his promise to his wife. He immediately telephoned Caroline Harmon at home, hoping to catch her there. She still worked, and he was not sure about the name of the architecture firm. Fortunately, when he called, she had just gotten home with her daughter. She had picked up the child from the church day care center and was home earlier than usual.

"Caroline, this is Carter Burns," he began. She was slightly out of breath when she answered. "You sound busy. How are you and that delightful daughter these days?" He went on to express his concern about certain legal matters. "I'm just calling to let you know I'm available to help in any way I can. All you have to do is ask." Before she could respond, he added, "I know it's difficult, Caroline. You've got quite a lot to go through. But a lot of people will help, if you just ask. Believe me. But you do need to do that. No one wants to butt in. But they'll fall all over themselves to be of assistance. In fact, you might have to put up a fence just to control the crowd," he added in a lighter tone. "Actually, you'll probably want to do more for yourself than they will let you. But that's healthy for you. You will be better off in the long run." Self-reliance was a subject on which Burns was an authority. As a reflex, he glanced at the plaque which read "Eagles fly alone."

She was grateful and said so. "Mr. Burns, I know what you're saying and I do, believe me, appreciate this call. I really haven't been putting things off. Kate demands so much of my time, and it's pretty much just me. You understand, I'm sure. You and Mrs. Burns have been so special. Always. I know I need to get the will thing started, and there's probably other things I haven't even thought about. I would love for you to help. And I do appreciate the prodding."

"Great. Why don't you call and make an appointment? I'll tell Mary, my secretary, to give you carte blanche, so long as it doesn't interfere with my golf," he laughed, wanting to keep the conversation light. He again encouraged her to call when she had the time and assured her one last time of his willingness to help.

* * *

A heavy rainstorm had moved into the downtown Raleigh area. From his office window Burns watched the storm approach from the west and was impressed by its intensity. He respected power in any form.

He had been on the telephone since returning from a noon meeting with Bob Henry regarding the headquarters location and its staffing. Henry had assured him that Greg Barlow's description of the building on Third Avenue had been everything he had envisioned they might need. Plenty of individual small offices, a large reception area, and easy access from the street. The location on a very busy intersection would provide excellent visibility. Burns was pleased with Henry's report and with Barlow's instincts about the location.

Mary Cole entered his office as he was hanging up with Henry. She handed him a note saying Kent Reed was holding on his private line. Burns ended his conversation with Henry and took the mayor's call as always.

"How's Charlotte holding up after our little dinner? Did the conversation scare her off?" Burns asked jokingly.

"No, she's having a field day. But her clothes bill could bankrupt me before the campaign even gets started" was the reply. "Hell, just the shoe bill alone looks like the national debt. Why do women have to have so many things for their feet? I've got three pairs of shoes, and they do just fine. I bet Charlotte has thirty if she has one."

"Don't worry about the money, Wedge," Burns said. "Leave that to Barlow and the rest of us. Your thoughts are needed elsewhere," he reminded his friend. Burns was ever the coach. "Now, what's on your mind? Surely you didn't call to talk about shoes."

"Frankly, I need to get away from the telephone, the press calls in particular. I was hoping you would meet me at Brookside for a little racketball in about an hour or so. You probably can get some time."

"Wedge, I wish to hell you had called earlier," Burns replied. "But Caroline Harmon called, and I'm meeting with her in about, oh, thirty minutes. She could need considerable time, if my guess is right. Besides, the damn rain doesn't seem to be getting any better. In this traffic it would take about an hour just to drive to the club. My best advice to you is that you get a massage, go home, take the telephone off the hook, and get some rest there. I'll call you on your other line, if I need you."

They talked further about the campaign, particularly the headquarters decision. Then the mayor followed the coach's advice and went straight home.

At four o'clock, Caroline Harmon arrived with her husband's will. She only brought a copy, since the original was still in the lock box at the bank. She had not had time to go by the bank on her way downtown. She came in holding a dripping raincoat and a small folder of papers. She was ushered immediately to Burns' office where he was looking through a file on another case.

"Caroline, I was pleased to get your call. Glad you could make it despite this weather," he greeted her warmly. She thanked him for staying late and handed him her accumulation of documents.

"Last night I gathered what I thought was important from Ken's desk at home. I've also written down a list of questions I didn't want to forget to ask."

She sipped slowly on the hot tea Burns's secretary had suggested when she first saw the drenched young woman enter the office. Burns carefully looked over the will first.

"This seems to be in order legally. There's nothing out of the ordinary." When she asked, he agreed to serve as coexecutor of the estate with her. The will had actually named Caroline as executrix, but she preferred to trust someone else with the details. They continued to discuss other matters in general with little emphasis on technicalities. He wanted to keep the first meeting as informal and uncluttered as possible.

When his secretary stuck her head in the door and said she was leaving, Caroline Harmon said it was late for her as well and she needed to get home. "Where'd you park?" he asked. "Are you in the building here?"

"No," she replied. "Rather than fight the traffic in this rain, I took a cab."

"Well, I'm on my way out, too. I'll drop you off at your house." She protested his generosity, but he insisted. "Nonsense, Caroline. It's on my way. Let me throw a few papers in the briefcase and we'll leave."

Considering the rain had only gotten heavier, she gladly accepted his offer. When they arrived at the Harmon residence on Valley Brook Road, Burns went in to speak to little Kate. He wanted to make sure the babysitter also had a way home, so Caroline would not have to drive her, especially with the small child. The sitter told him all she had to do was call her brother and he would pick her up.

That problem solved, Burns began to think about what had happened to Ken Harmon. "Caroline, as long as I'm here," he inquired, "would you mind showing me what you found when you came home and discovered Ken? I only want to settle in my own mind what occurred."

Thinking that was a good idea, she led the attorney into the kitchen where the door to the basement was located. She opened the basement door and turned on the light at the top of the stairs. Alone, he descended the steps and found the usual array of appliances, boxes, and crowded shelves. Burns looked at the clothes dryer and noticed that it was a Gem-X 400, a well-known brand in home appliances. He knew the manufacturer was located in the small town of Rocky Mount, North Carolina. The dryer had been moved to one side but otherwise untouched. The new dryer

CUNNING Treatment

did not appear to have ever been installed after the incident. The original carton was still in one corner of the basement. Caroline had been doing her laundry on weekends at her parents' home, so their maid could help.

Burns was satisfied with what he saw, but still had questions. Caroline was fixing some juice for Kate, and he asked her to recount as best she could the course of events that had preceded her husband's death. She briefly told him how Ken had purchased the dryer as a surprise and had insisted on installing it himself. The lawyer asked if the dryer had ever been turned on.

Caroline explained, "I've never used the dryer. I've been using the one at my parents' house, until I can call the appliance store to bring out another one and install it. I just don't feel right using the one downstairs."

Burns said he understood and complimented her judgment. He then thanked her for discussing the unfortunate events surrounding her husband's death. As he left, he apologized for asking unpleasant questions and promised to call her as soon as he was ready to place the will in probate. She promised to have the original will delivered to him, probably by her father, as soon as she could get to the bank.

* * *

Over the next several days, Caroline Harmon had little opportunity to think about her conversation with her old family friend and now attorney, Carter Burns. She did take time to retrieve Ken's will from the bank. She gave the document to her father, and Wink agreed to deliver it to Burns's office immediately. Otherwise, she was totally occupied with her new world of single parenting and the demands of her daughter. Partially out of uncertainty about the future and to a large degree because of the very real need she felt to have something else to distract her from her personal problems, Caroline decided to keep her job with the architectural firm a little longer. The hours were flexible enough to permit her to keep up with Kate's all-too-frequent reasons to stay home, but the work allowed her to escape the house often as well, to provide some sense of relief, however short-lived. She had early on resolved to allow Carter Burns to make all the decisions about legal matters. She trusted him and felt those things were just something else she did not want to worry about.

When the telephone rang, Caroline was in the kitchen. It was a Friday evening, and she had come home early that day. The daycare center had called her at work and said Kate's cold had gotten worse and she might have a fever. But they were not sure. The child refused to allow anyone to take her temperature except "my mommy."

The caller was Carter Burns. They had not spoken since their first meeting, when he had driven her home. He was again inquiring about the clothes dryer, which was still in her basement. "There isn't really more that I could tell you, Mr. Burns," she said. She was holding the receiver to her ear with her shoulder and struggling to wipe Kate's runny nose.

"Yes. It's still down there. I've called Ace Appliance twice, but they still haven't come after it. I do plan to get another one, but the one down there, as I told you the other day, I just don't want to use it," she explained. "Why do you ask? Do you think it's important?"

At that point the attorney recounted that he had carefully evaluated the assets provided her in her husband's will. Aside from the house and whatever equity could be established, it appeared that Ken Harmon had not updated his insurance coverage. "The bottom line is that not too far in the future, you and Kate might have to be very careful with finances," he advised. Frankly, Burns was surprised at the small size of Ken Harmon's estate value. But he contributed that to doctors' notoriously poor financial instincts and to the fact that apparently none of the pack of hotshot financial advisers had gotten to him before he died. But he did not share those opinions with his client.

"Oh, how well I know," she agreed. "Ken and I hadn't really worked with anyone to talk about our future finances. We were still struggling in many ways. He had the new practice and all that, and I had my job and Kate to think about. Buying this house was about the only decision he and I had really made of any substance. And I don't have to tell you that my parents are not as able to help as they once were. You know that, and you must understand why," she remarked. "But we can't change any of that now. Ken and I had talked about those things, more insurance and all that. He had made at least two appointments lately to get started on planning. But he had to cancel each time due to emergencies at the hospital. To be honest, we just weren't all that concerned. Other things seemed so much more important and demanding. Who would have ever dreamed anything like this might happen?"

"Actually, Caroline," the attorney continued, "I have been thinking about the dryer in the context of a lawsuit. I don't want to go into too much detail over the phone right now. But surely you've heard about products liability. Simply stated, the law says a manufacturer of a product has certain obligations to the consumer who buys and properly uses the product. If the manufacturer fails to meet those obligations, if he produces a defective product and it can be proven that the buyer's damages were related to the product's defect, well, you can sue the manufacturer. In your case the damages are the loss of your husband and Kate's father. And you did not just lose Ken the person, you lost his ability to provide income for you and Kate. As a promising plastic surgeon, that loss would no doubt be considerable."

There was a brief pause before she responded. "Are you saying that you could show that the clothes dryer caused Ken's death?"

"That's exactly what I'm thinking. At this point it's only a theory. But it's one we have to consider. From all indications, Ken was electrocuted. You told me that's what the paramedics said. That's probably what's on the death certificate, but I haven't seen it. If there's a reason the dryer caused the electrocution and it wasn't Ken's fault, a jury would be hard pressed to ignore the responsibility of the manufacturer." From experience Burns was confident the Harmon case could be a good one. A few years earlier, he had won a products liability case in which the plaintiff's case was not nearly as sound as the Harmon case appeared from all indications. He was reasonably confident the facts might be indisputable, if his investigation proved him correct. And so were his other conclusions. Caroline Harmon before a jury would be very effective. Proving Ken Harmon's value as a provider for his family would certainly not be a problem.

"Caroline, it's worth looking into. As I've explained, you do need to consider your finances. If you're entitled to damages, that is, money, from the clothes dryer manufacturer's insurance company, well, that's as good a source as any.

"Ken didn't have enough insurance. I can assure you that the dryer's manufacturer does," he stated matter-of-factly. "Believe me, Gem-X can afford it. And, quite honestly, you can't afford not to consider it. That's my best advice at this juncture."

"I understand what you're saying, Mr. Burns. I really appreciate all that you're doing. Just let me think about it a day or two. I'll call you back. Is there any urgency about doing any of this?" she asked.

"Legally, no. Not at this time. You have a year to file the suit. But for your personal needs, I recommend you act as quickly as possible. As soon as you feel comfortable with the idea, call me," he urged. "Most of the work will be on my part, but the go-ahead has to come from you. And don't worry about my fee. We'll let Gem-X worry about that."

"Thank you again, Mr. Burns. I'll try to do that," she said. "And I suppose I should keep the dryer for now."

"Absolutely. But I can have it picked up and stored, so you won't have to look at it every time you go into the basement. Just tell Ace Appliance. I believe you said they sold it to you or rather to Ken. Tell them to deliver a new one, and I'll get someone to pick up the other one."

When the conversation ended, she gazed out the kitchen window for a moment. She poured herself a glass of wine as Kate ran back into the kitchen demanding dinner. There was no doubt in her mind that Burns was right. She definitely needed the financial security a successful lawsuit could bring. She was painfully aware her parents were not able to help, and the architectural firm where she worked probably would not pay her more than they were already. What her attorney had just proposed was certainly worth considering. Of that and little else was she certain at that point.

CHAPTER 15

United States Highway 51 passed through the north side of Rocky Mount, North Carolina, and served as the primary connection between that town and Raleigh, some one hundred miles away. Just far enough to help the town fathers of Rocky Mount jealously guard its size. "Small Town America At Its Best" the sign said. And its character. "Safe For Our Families and Our Future" said the next sign at the city limits.

Passing two farmers' supply houses, five automobile dealerships, three supermarkets, a K-Mart, and one of Rocky Mount's two motels, Highway 51 proceeded through the town past the homes of the "old money" families, which sat grandly behind ancient oak trees and white picket fences. Next followed a small roadside park where "Help Keep Rocky Mount Clean" signs were posted near picnic tables. Right after the park came the entrances to Rolling Acres, Fox Hall Place, Country Estates, and other bastions of the town's "new money."

Just outside the city limits to the south were the corporate offices and manufacturing facilities of Gem-X, Inc.

Producing a line of home appliances, Gem-X had been Rocky Mount's primary employer since 1956, when the then family-owned plant had moved lock, stock, and barrel to the South from Akron, Ohio, to escape union organizers and utilize North Carolina's large population of cheap labor. The company had long enjoyed a reputation for quality manufacturing for which Rocky Mount was justly proud. Its reputation was jealously guarded by the old as well as the new money people who had all prospered greatly over the years.

In the early 1970s, Gem-X, Inc., had become a wholly-owned subsidiary of Standard Alliance Brands, Inc., the nation's second largest manufacturer of "white goods." The family's interests had been bought out by Standard, and family members had immediately fled Rocky Mount to more cosmopolitan climes. Despite the new influx of capital from Standard for expansion and equipment, the officers of Gem-X worked hard to maintain a large degree of independence from the parent corporation. Protecting that valued autonomy was practically a full-time preoccupation for many of Gem-X's top echelon and for good reasons. That protective attitude symbolized more than just the provincial thinking characteristic of so many small southern towns. More importantly the protective attitude sprang from a need, indeed an obsession, to save more than a few jobs of top Gem-X executives, whose free-wheeling business practices would have sent shock waves through Standard and its more conservative Board of Directors.

At age forty-nine, Hank Ralston had been Director of Customer Services at Gem-X, Inc., for almost twelve years. It was the best job he had ever had. A native of Rocky Mount, Ralston had previously sold real estate and then insurance before landing his job at Gem-X. It was the greatest thing that had ever happened to him, and he intended to keep the job at Gem-X at all costs. He was particularly proud of his work related to Gem-X's line of clothes dryers, which were manufactured and sold to distributors who marketed them nationally under three brand names, including the Gem-X name itself.

An early Monday morning in May found Hank Ralston walking into Steve White's office at Gem-X. At that particular moment, Paul Young, the vice president of finance, stopped Ralston and asked what he thought about the previous Friday's executive staff meeting.

"A lot of the usual crap," Ralston quickly snapped. "One damn thing's for sure. If Art Brooks doesn't get his shit together, that office will be vacant again. That loud-mouthed whale and his sales crowd had better shape up or the old man will be forced to roll another head. That is, if Bateman will let him," Ralston added with a slight snicker. He was referring to Carl Bateman, long time personnel vice president, who had run Gem-X for many years with an iron fist. Ralston knew Bateman utilized a network of corporate spies that would have made the K.G.B. look like Nixon's plumbers. Ralston continued his discourse on the general sales manager. "Brooks is an ex-jock who has lied his way to where he is. That has to catch up with anyone after just so long. It has to. He's a no-class jerk who keeps his nose up Bateman's skinny ass." Ralston was noted for his strong and usually accurate opinions about events and personnel at Gem-X. He glanced at Steve White, the recently hired young attorney, who was still waiting inside his office for Ralston's requested meeting. "I need to see Steve a minute, Paul. How about picking up some lunch today? I didn't bring my usual sandwich, so I'll need to go out," he offered. The two men agreed to meet in the parking lot at noon, as Young walked down the hallway to his own office.

Steve White was sitting behind his desk when Ralston finally entered the room and sat down. Having quickly gotten Clarence Darrow out of his system, White had practiced law privately only two years in Raleigh. That had been enough to convince him that a corporate practice held much more appeal than divorces, drunk-driving cases, and an occasional appointment to represent an indigent child abuser. When he had seen the advertisement in a Raleigh newspaper for a corporate attorney in Rocky Mount, White had quickly applied for and gotten the position with Gem-X.

"Steve, you know how seldom I ask you about one of these products liability suits or claims. You've got a good handle on them. But this one has gotten my attention," Ralston began. He laid a copy of *Harmon vs. Gem-X, Inc.* on White's desk. "Why are they suing for so damn much? I didn't read the whole thing. But five million dollars certainly caught my eye. That's one helluva lot of money," Ralston stated, obviously concerned.

"That one came in to me day before yesterday from Standard. They were served and forwarded it to me as usual. They probably

CUNNING Treatment

didn't even look at it. Some secretary does most of that work. But I did want you to see it. That's why I sent you this copy. All I know right now is what's in the complaint. After we choose outside counsel to represent us, we will be able to find out more about it once the discovery process starts," White explained. "I do know that the guy who died was a young doctor. That probably accounts for the large amount of damages."

The large majority of Gem-X's products liability cases arose from circumstances in which it could be proven that the consumer had misused the product. Those cases usually involved Gem-X's line of portable heaters, which were primarily used in trailers or small houses. Gem-X had almost always settled those cases out of court after the preliminary investigation pointed the finger back to the product user. No one could remember a death case involving a Gem-X product. And, certainly, there had been no substantial claims involving the clothes dryer line—ever. Only once had there been a problem with the dryers, and that was attributed to a faulty drain line which caused water damage and nothing more. The manufacturer of the drain tube had paid those claims, not Gem-X.

"Have you picked an attorney yet in this one?" Ralston wanted to know. The corporation always hired outside legal counsel to have the advantage of that counsel's malpractice insurance in case something went wrong. Gem-X looked after itself in all aspects.

"No, not yet. I was going to call Bill Houston today. The answer to the complaint is due in thirty days from last Wednesday. That gives us about three weeks," White informed him.

"Christ," Ralston snapped. "Houston is the last attorney you should appoint in this one." The local outside legal counsel in Rocky Mount was one of Ralston's favorite subjects of derision. "Houston only knows how to do taxes and cheat widows. That ass has no idea what a real lawsuit even looks like, much less how to handle it." Gem-X had Houston on retainer for small local matters in Rocky Mount. Houston had been the city attorney at one time and in Ralston's opinion had "raised ass-kissing to an art form."

"That's the best old Houston can do. He just stalls, blusters, and bluffs. He practices good-old-boy law at the Blue Ribbon Cafe and on the golf course. That may be fine for most things around here. But get him in a courtroom with real lawyers, and he wets his fucking shiny pants. I once heard a couple of years ago about a will contested by the dead man's second wife. It had gotten all the way to the State Supreme Court. Old Houston got up before the judges, the *Supreme* Court, mind you, and a whole room full of attorneys in Raleigh and, so help me God, talked about what a fine woman the dead man's *first* wife had been. Hell, she had been dead for ten years. Houston couldn't even discuss the case intelligently. All along he hadn't really had a case to defend. What he had done, though, was stall the will contest in discovery proceedings while the dead man's brother and son robbed the estate for themselves. And what the brother didn't get, Houston probably did. The widow was left with about $10,000 out of an estate worth about a quarter of a million in good farm land and a house she wasn't even allowed to enter after her husband died because the husband's two grown brats hated her guts. That's what Houston calls practicing law. Outside this town, he wouldn't get by with crap like that."

Being new to the company, Steve White wanted to know more. "How did Houston get the Gem-X business in the first place?" he asked.

"Well," Ralston began, all too eager to further cut Houston down to size, "Houston had brayed and bullied his way to the top in Rocky Mount. He always knows the right butt to kiss for something he wants. He and Carl Bateman are big golf buddies. But besides, if the problem needs a real lawyer, we always send it to someone in Raleigh which probably doesn't even bother Houston. In fact, he probably prefers it that way. He gets to act like a big shot around here and draw his retainer and doesn't have to show his ignorance in any matter of substance. We'll need a

CUNNING Treatment

son of a bitch for this Harmon case, but not a stupid son of a bitch like Houston."

White was always amused to hear Ralston on any subject, particularly someone on the inside like Houston. "How do you know all this about Bill Houston?"

"Steve, you can ask just about anybody. Personally, I know for a fact that he wrote wills for a city commissioner and the commissioner's wife here. Then he screwed them after they were dead. The commissioner had helped Houston get elected county judge at one time. Supposedly as a favor, Houston then drew up those wills and refused to bill them. Said he couldn't after all they had done for him. Well, after the commissioner died, Houston did a little legal work for the widow, all the while telling her he couldn't charge her. Said he loved her and her late husband too much. Shit. When the commissioner's wife died a few years later, old Houston presented her heirs and the estate a bill for over $7,500 for services rendered, including the damn wills. That repulsive bastard just crawled in line with all the other usual creditors with his slimy hand out. The widow and her husband both died thinking that jerk was a fucking saint."

"How do you know what happened? It sounds too personal to me," White remarked.

"To be honest, Houston probably doesn't know it. But the commissioner's wife was my aunt. Believe me. A lot of people know funny stories on our illustrious outside legal eagle."

"You've made your point, Hank. Do you already have someone in mind for the Harmon case?" White asked.

Ralston was thinking out loud. "This case was filed in Raleigh in circuit court. They had to do that even though Gem-X is owned by an out-of-state company, but a lot of the products liability laws are quirky. At least that's what I think. Raleigh's full of fancy, silk-stocking attorneys. I do have a lawyer friend in Raleigh. He might be just the one to handle this. His name is Harry Mills. He's about as shrewd as they come. Let me call him first, and then I'll give you his number. You can take it from there."

"Sounds good to me, Hank," White assured him, as Ralston left to return to his own office three doors down. Before leaving, Ralston again reminded White that he would tell him when to contact Mills.

∗ ∗ ∗

After several weeks, *Harmon vs. Gem-X, Inc.* remained a primary source of concern to certain individuals in the company. Steve White had sent the case to Ralston's friend, Harry Mills, when finally instructed and was waiting on the results from the preliminary investigation by Mills. Hank Ralston had only asked White about the progress a couple of times. Ralston felt comfortable with Mills and saw no need to panic about any inquiries from Standard regarding the lawsuit at that time. No questions had been asked, and he hoped they never would be. Accountability was not Hank Ralston's strong suit.

One morning Steve Young received a phone call. "Steve," the older man began, "this is Harry Mills from Raleigh. We've completed the deposition of Caroline Harmon. She's the widow of that young doctor in the clothes dryer case. And I must tell you, she makes a fine witness. A jury, if the case ever gets that far, will be impressed by her and what she has to say. I'll be sending you a copy of her deposition so you can judge for yourself. I may have missed something you can see, but the essential facts are clear. She has a damn good case."

"Sure. I'll give the deposition a thorough read. But, first, are we going to be able to see the clothes dryer?" White asked. "Do they still have it?"

"Oh, yes. The plaintiff's attorney has sent it to a laboratory for testing, with my approval, of course." Mills confirmed. "We can see it when the lab finishes and issues its report. But you know what that will mean."

"I'm afraid I do. From my experience, those paid experts can be simple prostitutes a lot of the time," White acknowledged.

CUNNING Treatment

"And people call lawyers hired guns," Mills laughed. "Some of those bastard experts agree with whoever is paying them every time. But I want your engineers to see the unit as soon as possible. You just be prepared for the worst. I will need to sit down with your people sometime soon to familiarize myself with the product. Can you arrange that? And you better send me the warranty information, the installation manual, and any other literature that goes out with one of those dryers. Make sure it's the same material for the same model as the Harmon case and a dryer as close as possible to the actual manufacture date for the Harmon dryer. I can review those prior to my inspection and before deposing the so-called experts."

"Be glad to, Mr. Mills. But our engineers will hate to see you coming. They have a heightened aversion to all lawyers. Even I can't even go around them without a chorus of groans, and I work here," White warned.

"Well, I'll be as easy on them as I can. I'm on their side. Remember to tell them that. Remind them of the difference, if you will. This one could be big. I want to move very carefully. The plaintiff's attorney is a political friend of the judge who will hear the case. That means we have to be doubly careful."

"I understand. Just give me a call and I'll set up any meeting you need with the engineers here," White said. "And do send me a copy of the Harmon woman's deposition."

Later that afternoon, Steve White reported his conversation with Mills to Hank Ralston. Ralston had come to the young attorney's office on other matters, but had asked about the Harmon case first. "Well, well," Ralston said, when he heard the part about the plaintiff's attorney being tight with the judge. "Looks like I'd better call Chuck Townsend. He's done some lobbying work for us at the state legislature. He might be able to give us some insight on what we're up against. Anyway, I would like to see what he knows about the judge and this lady's lawyer. What's the lawyer's name," Ralston asked.

"His name's on the complaint. Here it is. It's Carter Burns," White replied. He wrote the name down on a piece of paper and handed it to Ralston.

"Townsend could be helpful, Steve. It's worth asking," Ralston repeated as he left White's office. Definitely not prone to understatement, Ralston hoped this was not one of those rare instances when he was wrong. He was sure he needed all the help he could get. Chuck Townsend had been very reliable in the past and he might need to be again, Ralston acknowledged in light of what he had just heard.

CHAPTER 16

"Mother, will you keep Kate for a couple of hours this afternoon? I have an appointment with Dr. Robbins for a PAP smear, and I need to run by the hospital and check on Sally Matheson. She had her surgery yesterday," Caroline explained. "My regular sitter can't be here. She has a sore throat or something, and I don't want her around Kate." Ellen Collins's daughter rarely called on her mother to babysit, but she was in desperate need and took the risk. "Besides, you haven't seen the baby for days. She and I could use a little break from each other. She has to be bored having just me around." When her mother's response wasn't immediately positive, she decided to plead.

"Yes, I know this is Eadie's afternoon off. But it will only be for a couple of hours max. I promise. No more than that. Sally will be too tired from the mastectomy for me to stay too awfully long. And Dr. Robbins is very quick with those things. Please?"

At one o'clock that afternoon, Caroline drove up to her parents' home with Kate and a bag full of juices, Pampers, and a favorite teddy bear. They were met at the front door by the Collins's maid grinning ear to ear and reaching for Kate. "Eadie, isn't this your afternoon off?" Caroline protested, as the laughing black woman swept the child up in her arms.

"Yes, Caroline," Eadie replied, while she helped Kate off with her cotton sweater. The Collinses always kept the house much too warm in Eadie's opinion. "Don't you worry about that. I haven't seen this bunny rabbit for too long. I asked your mother if I could stay until you got through with your business." Caroline

CUNNING Treatment

suspected Eadie was slightly altering the truth about whose idea it was to have Eadie stay longer than usual.

"Where is Mother?" she inquired, sounding somewhat irritated.

"She's upstairs in her bedroom. Probably still asleep, so we'll stay down here, won't we Kate honey?" the maid said.

"You mean she's sleeping it off," Caroline snapped and glanced up the still empty stairway. "How bad is it this time?"

"Now, Caroline, you know you've got enough to do without concerning yourself about a grown woman. Your mother will be fine. Now, go on. You don't need to be late for your appointment. And, besides," she added, looking at the little girl in her arms, "I know where there are some fresh cookies, and they're not as good cold. We better hurry, bunny rabbit," she said. Kate immediately ran down the hall toward the kitchen with the maid chasing after her.

Caroline called to her as she disappeared down the hall. "Eadie, I'll be back by three o'clock. I'll be glad to take you home, so you won't have to catch the bus. I really appreciate this." But her offer was drowned out by the laughter and shrieks from the kitchen.

When Caroline returned to pick up her daughter, she found her parents in the study. Wink Collins jumped up from his leather wingback chair and warmly greeted his daughter at the door. "Come in, come in," he gestured and gave her a hug. "Eadie coaxed little Kate into a nap. She's still asleep up in your old bedroom." Caroline gave him a quick kiss on the cheek and walked over to sofa, sitting down on the opposite end from her mother, who smiled but said nothing. "Eadie will mix. No, I'll mix them myself. How about a martini or something?" Turning to his wife, he asked, "What's Eadie planning for dinner?"

"I thought Eadie was staying only until I got back," Caroline said.

"No, I'll be here through dinner tonight," the maid spoke up. "Kate helped me plan the menu. We all hoped you would be staying."

Leaning back, Caroline almost sighed. "Go ahead. Twist my arm. I'm sure Kate will be thrilled, and God knows I could use a break. Dad, how about a light Scotch? With lots of ice and a little water, unless it's Red Grouse and then leave off the water."

Returning from the wet bar, her father carefully handed Caroline a drink with some flourish and a cocktail napkin reading "Ya'll Come Back, Ya' Hear?" He reclaimed his chair from the cat and was pleased when Ellen finally spoke.

"How did things go with Sally?" she asked.

"Very well, I suppose. We couldn't really talk. There were people there from her church. I'll have to call her back for the details. Ken had warned me about her problem before he died. I told him about her mother. He wouldn't be surprised with Sally having the mastectomy. But she looked well. You know Sally. She's already planning a trip for right after the holidays. She'll drag Eric somewhere exotic and make him buy her everything in sight. That girl certainly has a way with men. But I still miss Greg. The four of us used to have so much fun. Now Sally's chased off Greg, and Ken's . . ." Her voice trailed off as she took a long sip of her drink.

"When was the last time you spoke with Carter Burns?" Wink asked. "I haven't seen him at the club lately at a time we could chat, and I hesitate to call him about your situation. I'm sure the two of you can more than handle things."

"Mr. Burns and I talk frequently. He's been wonderful to me. He's bending over backward with the lawsuit. He knows how much it means to Kate and me. The will's still in probate and will be for several more months. But we're doing fine," she said. "I've been able to reach certain funds from the estate. And with my job, we're doing fine."

At the other end of the sofa, her mother slowly shifted to face her daughter. Ellen was clutching a glass of bourbon. Her cocktail napkin in a tight wad fell to the floor unnoticed. "Caroline, you know how much it hurts us that we can't do more for you. Nowhere near as much as we want to. You must realize—"

"Mother, that's not necessary," Caroline interrupted. "In fact, I'd like to change the entire subject completely. I spend enough time as it is rehashing this whole thing," she said. "None of us needs that tonight. Okay?"

Before her mother could respond, Caroline asked about several of her mother's friends and anything else to keep away from what she knew her mother was dwelling on night and day. But on the way into the dining room where Eadie and a fully awake Kate had served dinner, Caroline felt she should reassure her parents that she still needed them. "Mom and Dad, if I need to discuss anything about all of this with you, I promise to do just that. I know you're concerned, and I do love you for that. It hasn't been easy for any of us. We're still a family and that's that," she finished with a quick kiss for each of them.

CHAPTER 17

The formal announcement of Kent Reed's candidacy for governor of North Carolina had been held up intentionally by Carter Burns, who had a definite purpose for everything. "We need to wait for Harris to announce first. Let the hoopla and shouting die down from that before we claim the limelight. Let's see what they do, what they have to say. Then we can use that to offer the voters a real contrast." And how right Burns was impressed everyone.

The official Stewart Harris announcement of his long anticipated candidacy in the Democratic primary was like every Harris political announcement ever made. Held in the old Harris hometown of Winchester, about sixty-five miles from Raleigh, the ceremony took place on a large flat-bed truck drawn up on the town square in front of the Jackson County courthouse. The truck bed and every light pole and parking meter around the square sported red, white, and blue bunting. North Carolina state flags flapped at each end of the truck bed, and a twelve-by-fourteen-foot poster of Stewart Harris's smiling face stood directly behind the podium. Several rows of folding chairs were set up on the ground in front of the truck bed, with many being reserved for traditional supporters of anyone named Harris. Behind them and on two sides a large crowd of well-wishers waved signs saying, "Harris for Governor" just as they had for his late father.

Before the speech began, there was an hour of entertainment to warm up the crowd. A local blue grass band worked the crowd into a frenzy with a repertoire that included "Carolina Comin' Home," "Rocky Top," and "Thank God, I'm a Country Boy," which was altered to say "Thank God, I'm a Harris Fan," Harris's campaign song. Emmie Maye Farnsworth, Miss Jackson County, had the honor of singing the song to the Harris supporters, the first time it had ever been heard in public. Next ensued precision square-dancing by the Corn Fritter Cloggers from the western part of the state, followed by the choir from the First Methodist Church of Winchester singing "God Bless America." Finally, the music subsided and all eyes were on the dignitaries on the platform.

Basically, it was a reunion for the Harris political machine. Next to Stewart and his wife, Alice, sat the nine-foot polar bear disguised as the candidate's Aunt Louise. Beside her sat Stewart's mother, Madeleine, beloved widow of former Governor Vernon Harris, along with former Commissioner of Education Howard Adams and former State Safety Commissioner Tom Ballard, a mountain of a man until he opened his mouth. On the other side of the platform were Jim Bob Campbell, four-term mayor of Winchester, and his wife, Tammy. Then there were four state senators and six state representatives from all sections of North Carolina, the black Baptist minister who would give the invocation, just as he had at Vernon Harris's last inauguration, and, finally, Chester Grubbs, the state's oldest living veteran, and his much younger third wife, Vera. Chester Grubbs would not miss a Harris rally or a chance to show off the lovely Vera.

As a special touch, no one introduced the candidate to the crowd. It was his idea. "They all know me," he declared. When the Reverend Jeremiah Cope said the last "amen" to the invocation, Harris just walked to the podium and said in the syrupy drawl that characterized the Harris clan, "I'm Stewart Harris. I'm running for governor of North Carolina." That dramatic announcement was followed by ten minutes of sustained cheers, applause, whistles, and one more rousing rendition of "Thank God I'm a Harris Fan." For the next twenty minutes the latest Harris candidate recounted his late father's accomplishments, deplored the state of affairs in the state, and vowed to carry on his father's legacy to achieve a better life for all citizens without giving a single clue regarding how he would do it.

And that was it. But that was all the Harris crowd ever needed. They then drove in a motorcade to the county park on the outskirts of Winchester where everyone devoured hot barbeque, baked beans, coleslaw, and cases of Mountain Dew. Hundreds lined up to tell the man-of-the-hour how much they thought of his father and how glad they were he was taking up the family mission.

* * *

Three weeks after the Harris announcement, written invitations were sent out to members of the news media across North Carolina. They were invited to the rotunda of the State Capitol Building at high noon at which time "His Honor the Mayor of Raleigh, The Honorable Kent Wallace Reed" would announce his candidacy for the top post in the state. He would only be accompanied by his wife, Charlotte. On the surface, the occasion belonged to the Reeds alone. Carter Burns had so decreed. In his brief message of seven hundred words, written by Burns as well, Reed promised to "seek out the best in all people of our great state, to listen to all who share our vision of the future, and to dedicate all my abilities to making North Carolina a rewarding place to live and grow and learn and prosper."

Copies of his remarks were passed out to the large crowd of members of the news media. There was no music. There were no cloggers. Most definitely, there were no "political retreads," as Burns called them. Before the local evening news, the same well-choreographed scene was played out for reporters in Charlotte and Asheville.

The desired comparison to the Harris announcement was remarkable and so noted.

It was clear to Reed insiders that Carter Burns had planned the entire event down to even the smallest detail. The quality of the paper for the invitation had to be just so, the print dignified. Charlotte Reed's suit was tailored perfectly, and Burns knew he could rely on her taste. The Reed message was simple, the words carefully chosen. There would be several weeks in which the lofty message could be expanded on, details given. Burns was ready to do that and even more.

CHAPTER 18

"Mary, get Judge Franklin for me," Burns instructed into the intercom. "If he's not available, leave word for him to call me at his earliest convenience."

Moments later Judge Warren Franklin was on the line for the attorney. "Caught you during a recess, I understand," Burns greeted him. "Well, this won't take too long, Warren."

"Take as long as you like, Carter," the judge replied. "That damned Arnold Hardesty is the defense attorney in this case. Apparently, he fully intends to give me a stroke before the day is over. A mistrial would be his best bet thus far. What's on your mind?"

"I think I can do you a favor," Burns began. "Is Al Gregory's son still a problem for you?"

"Calls every other day," the judge replied. "I expect to hear from his father any minute now, unless I do something."

"Well, I said a long time ago I would help, and I'm prepared to do that. Sorry it took so long, but I had to check out a few things to see where we might use him on a temporary basis," Burns apologized. "It looks as if we might need a first class go-fer to help Wedge during the campaign. We sure won't call it a 'go-fer' position, and it will be interesting, but that's essentially what it will amount to. That should get Gregory's kid off your back for a while. Since money's a big problem in the campaign right now, maybe this will jar loose some of Al's cash, if his son's involved in the campaign. Hell, the damn television spots are even more expensive than we thought they'd be. Anyway, doing

CUNNING Treatment

this might kill two birds with one job, so to speak. We need Al Sr.'s money, and you *don't* need Al Jr."

"By all means, Carter. That's the best news I've had lately." The judge was obviously relieved. "Are you going to contact young Al or his father first?"

"Probably see if I can catch both of them on the golf course at the same time. They usually play in the same foursome on Saturdays. I'll try to catch them this weekend. The sooner the better for both of us," he acknowledged. "I just wanted your opinion on this before doing anything." Burns knew he could have done as he pleased, but he enjoyed having any judge feel obligated to him.

"Proceed by all means. You don't know what a relief this is for me, Carter."

"Thank you, Warren. Think nothing of it," he lied. "Now you go back in there and give Hardesty a lesson in procedure he'll never forget," Burns said with an encouraging laugh and hung up. Within minutes he was calling Gregory Sr., not wanting to take a chance of missing him at the club. "Al, Carter Burns. Putting together a foursome for Saturday. Wondered if you and Al Jr., might join us. And I promise not to bring up the Binkley case, if you won't," he laughed. Earlier in the year Burns had trounced Gregory in a conflict of interest case involving two of Raleigh's most prominent bank officials. "Good. I'll see you both Saturday. If it suits, I've already arranged a nine o'clock tee time. I've heard you have one of those new graphite putters. Can't wait to see how it handles."

* * *

Days later when Burns and the mayor drove up to the front of the Hall Printing Building in Burns's new Lincoln, Bob Henry was already there sitting in his red '67 Mustang convertible and reading the newspaper while he waited. The attorney had called earlier in the day to tell Henry to meet them at the campaign headquarters at five o'clock that afternoon. The candidate and the campaign director wanted to look over the office space once more before they officially moved in and held the formal opening for the press.

The three men entered by the main door after Burns remarked about the excellent exposure the location provided. "This huge glass front will maybe show people how open the Reed candidacy intends to be. I like the fact it can be seen from all four corners of the intersection. Good job, Bob." Once inside Burns had questions. "Is there a back entrance? Ground floor. Surely, there is." Henry nodded "yes." "That's important. We'll need to be able to come and go without being seen every time. Sometimes privacy is crucial."

Walking down the long hallway, Burns let his companions know he had a few things on his mind, other than just office space. "There's a right way and a wrong way to run any headquarters operation," he began. "Wedge, if you don't mind, I'll give Bob a few thoughts on that subject," he said, knowing Reed would dutifully nod approval, which he did, and knowing once said it would be law. Burns then began the seminar.

"This backdoor is perfect. Gives us the ability to come and go, as I said, without a lot of attention. I'll want a small, private office for my own use, and I'm to have the only key. It needs to be close to the back entrance, and the door must not have glass," Burns directed. He paused before a locked door and tried the knob. "Check this one out. If it meets my requirements, this is the one." Walking further, he continued. "The only furniture in my office will be a desk, a lamp, three chairs—one behind the desk— a file cabinet that can be locked, and a telephone with a private line for my use only. Initially, we'll need at least five other lines for general headquarters use." Looking straight at Henry, he added, "And have the lines checked for bugs twice a week. We'll put in the expanded phone bank closer to the election."

By nature a cynic, hearing Burns's remark about telephone bugs, Henry wondered to himself whether Burns was a genius or just paranoid, but kept making notes on the legal pad he brought with him. He asked no questions at that point and was curious about Reed's silence, but again said nothing.

The three men then went through the rest of the offices that were unlocked on the first floor of the building. Throughout their tour, Burns shared his thoughts. "Wedge will have the largest office, suitably furnished, but not too elaborate. As headquarters manager, Bob, your office will be near the front door. That way you can see whatever goes on and whoever comes in. You'll need another office for maps and corkboards. Put a large table in the middle of that office, but no chairs. It's for working. No one sits down in a war room. There will be no liquor on the premises at any time," Burns stated emphatically. "And make damn sure the younger workers leave the funny weeds some place else. Anyone arrested during the campaign for anything gets fired immediately. I don't even want a fucking parking ticket connected with anyone associated with this operation."

As Reed proceeded to nod in agreement with every word, Henry continued making notes. However, he realized the "funny weeds" comment eliminated several of the city's more prominent people from positions in the campaign. Burns went on. "Bob, there are two million details to keep straight during all this. I've already spoken with Maggie Smith. She's no spring chicken, but she's willing to take charge of whatever we tell her to do. Maggie can be a great help to you, because of all the things she knows so well from previous campaigns around here. She's waiting for a call from you. Line her up as soon as possible and put her to work. You'll be damn glad you did." And she gives great head, Henry had heard. I bet Burns knows *that*, too, he thought.

At Burns's suggestion they left their cars parked in front of the soon-to-be-headquarters and walked the short two blocks to Casey's, a well-known watering hole. To Burns's way of thinking another great asset to the site. The attorney wanted to discuss other matters and thought a drink wouldn't hurt. What had begun as a tour of the headquarters site had evolved into a long journey through the orderly, precise mind of Carter Burns. It was the first such trip for Bob Henry, and he saw it as quite a demonstration of how Burns must have gotten where he was in life. He was impressed. Henry saw the reality of the coming weeks, perhaps for the first time. The afternoon was becoming an evening of confirmation for him. Confirmation that Burns was determined to put Reed in the governor's office. Henry wondered just how far Burns was willing to go to do that. He also acknowledged that the title of governor would belong to Reed, but the power would definitely belong only to Burns.

Once seated in Casey's at an out-of-the-way booth, Burns ran the gamut of a campaign checklist in a methodical, train-of-consciousness manner, discussing dozens of things that really mattered, particularly in his mind. On the subject of campaign literature, he demanded "final copy approval on all printed pieces, no matter how small or the cost. And the union stamp has to be on each piece. Period. Inventories have to be watched closely. Maggie will be good for that. Money is and will remain crucial. Too much money can be pissed away on poorly-controlled inventories of things like bumper stickers and yard signs. Don't overprint and don't mail extras with any order. Put one person in personal charge of the postage meter and give them a whip to use, if necessary. No private mail goes through the headquarters postage meter. Ever. Make sure everyone understands that."

Speeches. "I want to see each one," he ordered. "Consistency is important, and we don't want anyone's foot in their mouth over anything. There'll be three, maybe four standard speeches on certain subjects. Education is a big issue. The state's economy. Good balance between farm and industry concerns. The future in general. Stay away from taxes and don't get baited into discussing no-win issues like abortion rights. When you get a question from the press on something like that or anything, for that matter, you don't want to talk about, brush off the question and go immediately to something you *do* want to talk about. The press does not follow up, probably doesn't know how, or care from what I've seen." He paused to taste his gin and tonic. "Wedge, we'd better have a long session—and soon—on identifying the main issues and writing concise position papers on each one. I know a young political science instructor who can help us with those."

Burns took a longer sip of his drink and stared pensively ahead, saying nothing for a few moments. No one dared break the silence. Then he asked, "Did either of you ever really listen to one of Jimmy Carter's speeches? They're good examples of what I say must be avoided." Burns had been bitterly disappointed in President Carter's presidency and blamed a great deal of what he perceived as a failure on the president's simplistic, homey method of communication. But there was an even bigger fault in Burns's opinion. "Not Carter's press conferences, particularly, but his speeches. Take that acceptance speech at the 1980 Democratic convention in New York. Pure, meaningless fluff and not even interesting fluff at that. But that's not the only problem as I saw it. Do you know what was so wrong with what he said?" Burns's answer to his own question surprised at least Bob Henry.

"Too many *I's*. Jimmy Carter said 'I have done this' and 'I have done that' and 'I will do this' or at least that's what I heard." Burns gave heavy emphasis to each *I*. "It was never *we* or *this administration*. The man appeared to be self-consumed and that's what hurt him. It was his obvious decency that got him elected. Had there been no Nixon and Watergate, there would have been no Jimmy Carter in the White House. Jimmy Carter is a wonderful, caring man. There's no doubt he's damned intelligent. But that damn speech almost made him sound like more of an egomaniac than Richard Nixon." Burns was insistent. "You have to give the people listening a shared feeling of identity. A shared mission. It has to be *we* not *I*. A man with too many *I's* is blind. That's pure and simple truth. Remember that, Bob. Remember that." Bob Henry was certain he would. Basically, Burns was dead right. "It's the *We're all in this together, North Carolina* that gets people's attention and loyalty."

On people around Reed. "Stewart Harris is going to parade around the state always in the company of local hacks, the over-the-hill gang if ever there was one. We don't need that. We need the endorsements of certain people, but we don't want them out front. They carry too much baggage with them, too many liabilities. Some of them will help us privately. They'll be content to do that if handled correctly, and that's one of my main functions in this whole thing. They have a few enemies of their own, and we sure as hell don't want to share them."

The waiter brought another round of drinks and Burns continued. "Wedge, when you're out in the territories, keep one or two young clean-cut types with you. One needs to be a female. That's the image we want. Fresh. Independent. Business-like. No huge entourage. The people of North Carolina will be your entourage. That image is part of the message."

Henry laughed to himself. He thought, sitting in that booth at Casey's, the three of them must have resembled the children's story characters Wynken, Blynken, and Nod. Burns, Henry, and Reed—in that order.

After the lengthy meeting, Burns returned to his law office where he found exactly what he had hoped would be there. His secretary frequently taped important—really important—messages to the back of his desk chair where they couldn't be missed. There was one such message that evening. He crossed the room and removed the piece of yellow paper from the back of the chair, being careful not to let the tape tear it. He was pleased to see that Lenore Fowler had returned his call from the previous day. She was one aspect of the Reed campaign only he could handle, and the sooner the better, he knew. Looking at his watch and seeing that it was past ten o'clock, he decided to wait until the next morning to speak with Lenore Fowler, mother of Senator Kip Fowler and still very much an influence in North Carolina politics. Burns was calling the powerful Lenore to arrange a meeting. Its sole purpose was to neutralize her in the governor's race. And he was confident he had the means to have his way.

Early the next morning, early even for Carter Burns, he was in his office before Mary Cole arrived. When she did enter the office suite and realized her boss was already sitting at this desk, she quickly made the coffee. She brought him his first cup, never decaffeinated, along with the morning newspaper he preferred to see before anyone else. "Thanks for the coffee, Mary. I would have started it myself, but you remember how bad it was the last time I tried that," he said. "Wait another half hour and then see if you can get Lenore Fowler for me. If we catch her early enough, she should still be at the farm."

When the call was placed, Lenore Fowler was gracious to the secretary and said not to worry about the early hour. "I've already walked three miles and inspected two new colts Jonathan bought last week in Tennessee. Rest assured your boss will have to get up even earlier to catch me napping. Put him on."

"Well, Lenore," Burns began when he finally picked up the receiver, "we know the sun never used to set on the British Empire. From all indication, you're doing your darnedest to keep up that tradition."

She laughed, and he knew she loved his flattery. After a few moments of pleasant banter, he proposed and she accepted a meeting for the next day. "I would suggest you come into the city and have lunch, Lenore, but if it's the all the same for you, I'll just drive out to your place. It won't take long."

"It will only be me, Carter. Jonathan has a doctor's appointment in Raleigh and should be tied up with that and other things most of the day."

"That's fine," he said, pleased he would not have to work to get her alone for what he had to say. "I'll be there at ten o'clock, if that's suitable for your schedule."

"I have no schedule when I'm at the farm, Carter. Ten will be fine."

CHAPTER 19

Being the state capital, Raleigh was blessed with a vast assortment of monuments and revered institutions dedicated to the betterment of the people of the state and honoring a proud history. But Casey's was a monument of quite a different variety.

Named after a legendary Speaker of the State Senate in the 1930s and 1940s, Casey's housed a superb restaurant and a richly decorated pub, never referred to as a *bar* by the natives. When Senator John Patrick Casey died of a heart attack while visiting his ancestral home in Dublin, his fellow senators and loyal supporters who had benefited during his "reign" wanted to make a lasting and appropriate contribution to the powerful man's legacy. So several of them formed a limited partnership, and Casey's was born.

Housed in a turn-of-the-century three-story brownstone on the National Register for Historic Buildings, Casey's was a sumptuous collection of wingback chairs in rich earth tones and burgundy leather, walnut breakfronts filled with leather-bound volumes and Irish porcelain, red leather stools and captain chairs in the pub, pegged dark oak floors throughout, and numerous hunt scenes with faint lights adorning their frames. In the pub itself, on the first floor of the old house, a massive fieldstone fireplace burned year round. On the second and third floors, the small, individual dining rooms were warmed by brass chandeliers and candle sconces on the walls. The marble entrance way on the street level presented a display of various memorabilia of the late Senator Casey. Each guest was greeted by a life-size oil portrait of the man himself standing beside a favorite horse famous for steeplechase victories throughout the eastern United States. A sister painting hung in the Hunt Room of the Brookside Country Club where Senator Casey had been a founding member.

The restaurant's entree menu offered lobster, prime rib, and Cornish game hens with fresh vegetables from local farmers who had long benefited from Senator Casey's ability to "get things done" for them. The impressive wine list was rivaled only by the extensive variety of Scotch and Irish whiskies. Around the perimeter of the pub, paneled booths provided convenient, private rendezvous sites for many politicians and business types. Many a career and many a deal were made or broken in a booth at Casey's. Insiders knew that was just the way the senator would have liked it.

Hank Ralston and Chuck Townsend occupied one of the booths at Casey's late one afternoon two months after the death of Dr. Kenneth Harmon. The meeting had been sought by Ralston right after he got word about the Harmon lawsuit. Over the telephone he had briefly described the case's background to Townsend, but asked to meet face to face to explain what he was after.

"They certainly didn't waste any time filing the suit," Townsend commented. "Any indication the widow might be in trouble financially? Usually these things take longer to get filed. Does Gem-X have many like this one?"

"No, not at all. At least not for damages this big. And that's what bothers me," Ralston explained. "We try not to attract our parent corporation's attention, especially not this way. Quite honestly, we should have put those damn ground wire warning labels on that dryer model some time ago. But we were trying to control costs, and recalling the dryers would have been expensive and costly to the product line in more than one way." Taking a sip of his Manhattan, he elaborated on his dilemma. "Those bastards will have my ass if this comes to light. I can't afford to take the fall for this screw-up."

Ralston was more nervous than his lobbyist friend had ever seen him. "Okay," Townsend said, as he bobbed the olive in his martini with one finger. "What business is all this of mine?"

"Do you know an attorney named Carter Burns? He practices here in Raleigh," Ralston asked.

"Sure. I've met him a few times. He's one of the top legal eagles around. And lately he's become something of a political wheeler-dealer. From all indications he has big plans for Kent Reed. He's the mayor of Raleigh right now. Wants to be governor. Is Burns involved in this lawsuit?"

"Burns represents the widow in the damn thing. How well do you know him? I know you said you've met him. But have you actually dealt with him before, not just socially? Just how do you know him?"

Townsend paused and then laughed. "I think I know where this conversation is headed. And, my friend, you don't have that kind of money. At least, I don't think so. I could be wrong. Got a Cayman account you've never mentioned before?"

"Just one goddamn minute, Chuck," Ralston shot back. "I'll decide that. I just need for you to look into this. Find out how much 'that much' really is, as you put it."

"Do you realize what you're asking me?" Townsend said with some irritation mixed with disbelief. "Burns isn't your usual hired gun. He's a strong influence in some pretty powerful circles in this town." But he saw that Ralston was not going to be bluffed easily. The stakes were too high. Gem-X and Ralston had something big to hide, and Ralston was determined to accomplish that no matter what.

"All I'm asking is that you give this situation and all the players some careful thought," Ralston stated in a low tone. "Just let me know if there's anything that can be done. That's all. I'm not asking you to actually do anything at this point. It's still early in this thing. Just think about it. That's all."

"All right, Hank. I can do that much. But this has to be the damnedest thing I've heard in a long time. Sure I couldn't just get you laid and forget about this lawsuit crap?" Townsend said, very seriously.

"You sure as hell can get me laid, old buddy," Ralston replied with some relief. "But don't forget about any of this for one minute. It's important to a lot of people, not only me."

"One more drink and let's go," Townsend said reluctantly, signifying his acquiescence, his agreement to see if anything could be done and how to approach doing it.

* * *

Hank Ralston was in his office at Gem-X, Inc., when he received Chuck Townsend's message to meet him back at Casey's. Several days had passed since their initial meeting about the Harmon lawsuit. Ralston quickly canceled his afternoon appointments and drove to Raleigh. He was nervously waiting in a booth in the famous pub when Townsend suddenly appeared from another part of the room with a drink already in hand.

Ralston had not seen his lobbyist friend when he settled into one of the restaurant's secluded leather booths. Townsend's sudden appearance startled him. "Sorry if I kept you waiting. I was just over there talking with John Fogel. He's a congressman from Pennsylvania," Townsend explained, as he slid into the booth opposite Ralston. "The word is Fogel's in town to meet with Kip Fowler. Wants to discuss the Democratic ticket for next year. Wants to do a salvage job on the party after Mondale's humiliating defeat. If you're ever running for president, don't ever tell people you're going to raise their taxes. Talk about a death wish." Townsend considered himself a politico of exceptional skill and finesse. For him the ultimate rush was being on the inside of whatever was going on. "Kip's still recovering from that surgery after the plane crash. Isn't able to travel much just yet. So some bigwigs are coming to see him here. Looks interesting for him, to say the least."

"No problem," Ralston lied. "I haven't been here long at all. That damn interstate construction is a real mess. And on top of that, some hotshot state trooper was pulling people over right and left. Guess the jerk has a quota to meet. Stupid hot dog."

"Christ. You're in a great mood. Think I'll go back to The Pride of South Pennsylvania. All the congressman wants is to be president. On the other hand, all you want me to do is bribe the most powerful attorney around here," Townsend said with comic exasperation.

Ralston jumped at the opening. "Okay, wiseass. Since you brought up the subject, what the hell have you found out?" he demanded. A waiter passed, and Ralston motioned for drinks for himself and the man who he hoped had all the answers.

The lobbyist sat back and nonchalantly gave his report. "Well, it's a long shot at best, but there is an angle worth considering if you're interested. And have the guts," he added, seriously eyeing Ralston.

"That's for me to decide," Ralston said and leaned forward in his seat. Bottom line, he knew guts also meant money. Probably a great deal of money. He wanted to hear more. "What exactly are we looking at?"

"We all know Carter Burns is a political pro. It's also getting to be known in some circles that he wants very much to be the next North Carolina Attorney General. He wants it badly, so I understand."

"Go on."

"It seems Burns has all his eggs in one basket. That's his buddy Kent Reed, the mayor of Raleigh. Burns is running Reed's campaign for governor from his private law office. Reed's his ticket to the A.G.'s office, pure and simple. But Reed has to win first, and that may not be all that easy."

"What's standing in his way?"

"It's not just so much what, but who. The who is Stewart Harris. The 'what' is money, and that's where you come in."

"Surely he doesn't think Harris is that formidable," Ralston remarked. Harris's shortcomings were well-known.

"No. They know him pretty well. But he's still a problem. They're just not sure how much of a problem he is at this time. They're not willing to take any chances. Harris is young. He's going for it full speed. There are a lot of people who still remember his father. Bet there could be not just a few powerful chits for him to call in out there."

"Which one has the inside track?" Ralston wanted to know.

"A whole bunch of folks resent the hell out of the fact that Stewart Harris's aunt might end up running things again. They damn well know she might call all the shots after the election. If her nephew wins, that is. Just like she did during her brother's last term in office, when she held court from her secluded office on the second floor of the State Capitol. The one with the only private bathroom in the whole fucking building. That woman had to be reckoned with if you wanted anything. Anything. And her nephew's a poor replica of his father. Only minus his father's charisma and several inches in height, I might add."

The obviously knowledgeable lobbyist continued. "But Reed has his problems, too, the chief one being funds, if what I hear is correct. He's got to have plenty of funds to get his name out across the state. Television time is expensive. But it's essential to Reed. He's not too well known outside the immediate Raleigh area."

"How bad is their money problem?" Ralston pursued.

"That I don't exactly have a feel for right now. You have to decide what it's worth for me to even find out." There it was. The bottom line for Ralston to deal with.

"Do you really think a campaign contribution could bury this damn lawsuit?" Ralston asked somewhat skeptically.

"Not a contribution per se. The campaign funding laws would be too strict on that angle. Too much scrutiny. But that's where the need is, for sure. You've just got to find a way to accomplish that with as few strings as possible. That is, if this crazy idea of yours has any appeal to Burns at all." Townsend was still very leery about the whole idea.

"How do you go about finding out what's possible with Burns?" Ralston would not let go. Too much was riding on it.

"I can't go to Reed. And I sure as hell can't go to Carter Burns. I don't even know him that well. But I do know a guy named Greg Barlow. He's pretty damned close to both of them. He's working in the Reed campaign. I think he might even be treasurer. Barlow's a young attorney in Raleigh, but that's nothing to be afraid of. I could approach him and at least plant the thought in his head. See what he does with it, if anything."

"What will that cost me?" Ralston asked, knowing there was always a price tag.

"I thought Gem-X's money would be footing the bill," Townsend inquired.

"Sure, it's Gem-X's money. But there's a limit to what I can bury in any account." He took a long swallow of his drink. "I can give you one thousand dollars—for you—to go fishing. If it works, there'll be more. But I need an answer by next week."

"You'll get one. At least an answer to the basic question," Townsend assured him. "And I want that thousand dollars now. I keep that, no matter what."

Ralston agreed. "A young guy from my office will meet you here tomorrow at this same time with your money. His name is White. He'll have an envelope with him, but he won't know what's in it. Don't open it here, and don't discuss anything with him. I'll make up something, and he'll believe it or go to work somewhere else."

As they left the booth at Casey's, Townsend promised to call Ralston as soon as he had something to report. "But no later than the next week," Ralston reminded him. He watched as Townsend wandered back in the direction of Congressman Fogel's booth. Ralston knew every aspect of the whole idea, including Townsend, was a big risk. He was also convinced he would take it.

* * *

CUNNING Treatment

Paul Young, Gem-X's vice president of finance, was waiting in Hank Ralston's office when he returned from their regular Monday morning senior staff meeting. It had not yet been a week since Ralston's meeting with Chuck Townsend in Raleigh.

"Hi, Paul. Sorry about lunch the other day," Ralston said, as he tossed a large stack of papers onto his desk, upsetting his calendar and sending it crashing to the floor. He picked up the calendar and began straightening the papers. "I had to go to Raleigh on the spur of the moment."

"Hell, I don't even remember what day you're talking about. I was probably tied up myself. Don't worry about it. But I do still need to get your opinion on something. And it has to be in confidence. It can't leave this office."

"Go ahead. What's up?" Ralston asked, interested.

"Let me shut the door," Young said and moved quickly to do just that.

"Must be a real problem. Sure you want to start off the week this way?" Ralston questioned flippantly.

"I don't have any choice. Just wish to hell I did. But this one won't go away that easily."

Ralston saw his visitor was serious. Finance people rarely joked about business. He knew that from past experiences. "What happened? Did you fuck up an audit?"

"Not even that simple, I'm afraid." Young lowered his voice, even though the door was shut. "It's Carl Bateman. I'm not sure I can handle him or not. Even whether anyone should try."

"What's the Skinny Godfather done this time?" Ralston queried. He leaned back in his chair and folded his hands behind his head. His relaxed posture belied his concern. He had learned to always be wary of Carl Bateman, the company's all-powerful vice president of personnel, who seemingly had the longevity of Rameses II and the ego to match.

Young went further with his story. "Who's been at Gem-X since it opened its doors down here in Rocky Mount?" he asked.

"Carl Bateman" was Ralston's quick answer. "He's controlled personnel since day one."

"Who's fired everyone that ever mattered around here? People at all levels. When a head rolled, who did it?"

"Carl Bateman" was again the response. "He takes a great deal of pleasure in telling people that no one can be fired without his approval. The guy's a fucking vulture. But we've been over that subject enough before. What's he done this time that has you so concerned? Any of your troops turning on you?" Ralston knew Carl Bateman had a ring of loyal spies in every division of the company. The finance division was no exception.

"I just want to make sure you understand a few things or at least remind you. One more question. Corporate titles aside, who actually runs Gem-X?"

"For Christ's sake, Paul. Bateman. Bateman. Bateman." He leaned forward in his chair to give emphasis to the name. "That asshole Phillips—and I do mean asshole, stupid asshole at that—Phillips thinks he does. Standard sent Phillips down here to run things, probably to shape things up so they could unload it, unless I miss my guess. But Phillips is just a pawn. Bateman is still numero uno. Standard knows that. Has all along. So what else is new?"

"Okay. Just so I know you understand. And you know Bateman has no love lost where you're concerned," Young reminded him. He wanted to erase any notion Ralston had that he was unaffected by anything Bateman did.

Ralston willingly acknowledged the fact. "Oh, that's a given. But that's nothing I can't handle, if ever I need to."

Famous last words, Young thought to himself, then continued. "The other day that wiry little bastard slithered into my office with a cigarette in each hand. Seems he had found out I was planning to audit two of our oldest and biggest vendors. Standard requires periodic audits, and I had decided this year to audit our accounts with Master Impressions and World Skyways. It had been a while since either had been looked at, if ever seriously." Master Impressions performed a large portion of printing for Gem-X, while World Skyways handled all special travel in the

United States and overseas for Gem-X executives and distributors.

He elaborated further. "During the last fiscal year, Gem-X spent over a half million dollars with Master Impressions just printing stupid in-house crap. World Skyways took in over two million for its services during the same period."

"So?"

"Well, when he got to my office, Bateman was smoldering over both prospects," Young stated.

"What in hell does the vice president of personnel have to do with printing and travel for the entire company? They're the Sales Division's suppliers, anyway."

"That's the magic question, my friend."

"Go on, Paul. What did Bateman say to you?"

"In the period of about half an hour and at least half a pack of cigarettes, Bateman carefully reviewed with me the history of my predecessors. And in each case he let me know that whenever the boat was rocked regarding either Master Impressions or World Skyways, one of my predecessors was soon missing from the ranks of Gem-X. He didn't actually threaten me, but he was being as subtle as the snake he is."

Ralston was suddenly looking at Young very carefully. "What did you say to him?"

"I listened to what he had to say. Told him I would check into the real necessity of those audits at this time. I may have even tried to suggest that the timing of the audits had been made by someone else in the division. I just played dumb."

"So you backed down."

"What the hell else could I do? That son of a bitch had my balls by both hands and was letting me know he would pull at will."

"I thought you said he had a cigarette in each hand. Did it burn them?" Ralston was trying to lighten the moment. It didn't work.

"Screw it, Hank. You know what I mean. He's hiding something from the big boys at Standard. Hell, he's hiding it from everyone. Has been for years. He protects those two accounts as much as possible. I've heard that Bateman is the silent partner in Master Impressions and gets his share of the profits on a regular basis. He makes sure a hefty chunk of our printing business goes right to Master Impressions. An audit would show that in a flash."

"I know. I've heard those stories ever since I've been here. And he does protect those accounts. No doubt about that. But he could be saving the company some money. Who can tell?" Ralston was then thinking about the Harmon lawsuit and how he was protecting that particular matter from the prying, critical eyes at Standard. Ralston and Bateman had more in common than Paul Young knew.

"I had called that fool Art Brooks and casually asked him if he had any problems with any of his suppliers in Sales. Just generally inquiring about the corporate relationships with vendors. I hadn't mentioned either Master Impressions or World Skyways by name at that point. Of course, he said everything was just fine. Only then did I ask him about the three invoices he had approved for over one hundred and sixty-five thousand dollars for paper purchased by Master Impressions three months ago. For paper which, by the way, was never purchased. That's what brought that account to my attention. Our people went down there, and there was no stockpile of paper in Master Impressions' warehouse when we needed those brochures at the last moment. But we sure as hell had paid for it months earlier."

"What did our brilliant VP of sales have to say about that?" Ralston did not hide his sarcasm and dislike for the blowhard Art Brooks, who, he long suspected, was one of Bateman's toadies.

"Brooks calmly assured me that those purchases had been approved in advance by the vice president of personnel, and he hadn't questioned the invoices when they crossed his desk for his signature. He did allow that Bateman had alerted him to the invoices before they arrived and told him not to be concerned. Brooks is painfully aware there's a graveyard full of his predecessors as well. Rest assured, Bateman didn't have to waste his breath reminding Brooks of that fact, either."

"Christ. You might say all that stinks," Ralston said, trying to show some sympathy.

"Thought I would get your attention. Skyways is easy to ignore. There's so much going on in that account. Big bucks all around. But Master Impressions is different, a much smaller operation. The size of those paper invoices would get anyone's attention."

"Now what are you going to do?" Ralston leaned back again in his chair waiting for an answer.

"At this point, Hank, I honestly do not know. I did postpone those audits for the time being. But how long can this crap go on without someone at Standard finding out and dragging us all down?"

"What makes you think someone at Standard doesn't already know?" Ralston posed cynically.

Young was incredulous. "Jesus Christ! Do you think Phillips knows about Bateman's set up?"

"Sure, Paul. Phillips isn't too deep in the head department. He may have a law degree, but that doesn't make him a genius by any means or even honest. He talks a good game and may even be a nice guy at home. But he's no match for Carl Bateman. No, sir." Ralston sat forward to continue his seminar on life at Gem-X and its parent, Standard Appliance. "Phillips was sent down here from Standard to straighten things out, but not necessarily all things. He's a hatchet man, nothing more. He doesn't understand a damn thing about this business, this industry. But, hell, when he got here, he found out Bateman's got a bigger hatchet than he does. That skinny bastard has a long history with Standard. Phillips had to be scared shitless. Someone at Standard has to be protecting Bateman all these years. Even as stupid as he is, Phillips had to pick up on Bateman and his peculiar interest in Master Impressions and World Skyways. But he couldn't say a damn thing."

Young had to agree. "Nobody on God's green earth knows why the head of the personnel division would have total control over company printing. Or a half dozen other pies he's got his fingers in."

"Paul, the man's a master. He's got Phillips totally bluffed. Don't forget that. When Bateman decides someone has to go, especially if someone gets too close to the Master Impressions thing, the bastard invents a couple of reasons and gets one or two of his toadies to verify some cock-and-bull story. And if that's not enough, he finishes off the victim with innuendoes about some broad stashed somewhere. The man's a damned psychotic liar with no conscience. It doesn't matter to him who gets hurt."

"Bateman sure did a number on Hal Bryson. That's one good man he chased out the door. And that stupid Chet Moses kisses Bateman's butt and keeps the rumor mills running day and night. When Bateman gets someone, you can bet your last dollar Moses threw more than one of the knives. He's about as bright as a firefly, that pious redneck. But old Bateman plays him for all he's worth around here. Chet Moses and Art Brooks are both Bateman's private brand of poison." Young paused for a moment to reflect on what had initially brought him to Hank Ralston's office. "And now he's breathing down my neck."

"Relax, Paul. Go along for now. If Bateman wants you to keep your hands off his little kingdom, I suggest you do just that. This mess has cost the company too many good men already. It's not worth your head rolling over it," Ralston advised.

Before Young could agree or protest further, Ralston's telephone rang. His secretary told him he had a long distance call from "a Mr. Chuck Townsend in Raleigh." Covering the receiver with his hand, Ralston told Paul Young he needed to take the call, indicating it was private. "Look, Paul, take my advice. Cool it with Bateman and those damned audits. Let's get together tomorrow if we can. Let me know if I need to do anything for you in the meanwhile."

As soon as Young shut the door to the office, Ralston told his secretary to put the call through. After a brief discussion, he agreed to meet Townsend in Raleigh the following afternoon. Again at Casey's. Ralston wanted results. His conversation with

Paul Young had made him even more apprehensive about the Harmon lawsuit. He could imagine the consequences if he didn't manage to defuse that bomb, and the sooner the better.

However, the meeting with Young had not been wasted. For Ralston it had been definitely productive. The whole time they had been talking, he had been intrigued with how Bateman used a corporate account to line his own pockets. A lot of money could be buried in the right account, if someone planned it very cautiously. And Ralston thought he knew just how to do it. He wanted first to meet Chuck Townsend to see what he had learned from his meeting with Greg Barlow. Then he would make his move.

The next day at Casey's Ralston laid out his plan for Townsend one step at a time. First, Townsend confirmed to him that Kent Reed's campaign advertising was being handled by the Edmundson Agency in Raleigh. That was just as Ralston had hoped. The Edmundson Agency also did the national media advertising for Gem-X, and Ralston controlled the corporate advertising division. Over the years he had learned how those accounts could be manipulated to hide many expenses which were never to be seen by Gem-X. Bert Edmundson, the savvy head of Raleigh's largest advertising and public relations agency, personally oversaw the Gem-X account. He had been a willing participant in the deception before. Ralston was confident he would be more than willing to go along again in order to keep the account.

"Are you sure the Reed campaign isn't wallowing in money?" he asked Townsend over their second drink.

"Sure, I'm sure. No campaign ever thinks it has enough money. That's the lifeline of the whole operation."

That was all Hank Ralston needed to hear at that moment. It would be simple for him to use Gem-X's advertising account to pay for campaign advertising produced and placed for Reed by the Edmundson Agency. He knew Bert Edmundson would cooperate. He would offer seventy-five thousand dollars for Carter Burns's candidate. It would be up to Chuck Townsend to see whether or not Burns was in a bargaining mood.

CHAPTER 20

It was about 6:30 P.M. Carter Burns was putting some papers into his briefcase when his private line summoned him back to his desk. The caller was Greg Barlow.

Burns told him he was preparing to leave for a meeting. However, he agreed to wait, if Barlow was coming right over, as he said he would. Anyway, Barlow sounded very excited about something he needed to discuss immediately.

"What's the problem, Greg?" Burns asked when the young attorney entered his office slightly out of breath. "Campaign treasurers usually don't get so excited. They leave that for us mules," Burns joked.

Barlow went right to the point. "Are you acquainted with an attorney named Chuck Townsend? He's a lobbyist. You may have seen him around during legislative sessions," Barlow inquired.

"I don't know him personally. But yes, I know who he is. We've met on a few occasions at social functions when the legislature's in town. Is he why you're here?" Burns asked bluntly, and without pausing asked further, "what's he after and what will it cost us?" Burns knew lobbyists were always after something or somebody.

"What makes you think it's something like that?" Barlow replied defensively.

"Greg, Townsend's a lobbyist. Those guys are always doing a favor for someone, and it usually carries a price tag, some small and some not so small. If Townsend were sitting here right now himself, I'd ask the same damn question. It's the nature of the animal he is. Townsend's no different than all the rest. Has he spoken with you about something?"

Barlow saw that Burns was ready for a story and decided to lay out the whole scenario. "Townsend called me at my office this morning, a couple of hours ago. He asked me to meet him for a beer at Casey's this afternoon, and I did. That's where I was when I called you," he began. Burns was listening, but looked at his watch and reached to turn on the local news. Barlow continued. "Townsend might have some money for Reed's campaign." He was certain that would get Burns's attention. And it did.

"Well, he sure called the right person for that. You are the campaign treasurer. Nothing wrong with that. What kind of money is he talking about? Where's it coming from?" Burns wanted to know.

"Seventy-five thousand dollars. He said it wasn't in cash. That his client was willing to hide that amount for campaign advertising costs. His client's a corporation," he clarified.

"Who's he talking about and why so much?"

Barlow was ready with the details. "Townsend's speaking for a fellow at Gem-X Corporation. They're located over in Rocky Mount."

"I know who they are," Burns assured him. "Make appliances." At which point, Burns immediately thought about Caroline Harmon's dryer, but said nothing.

"Townsend wants to make a campaign contribution, only it can't be known. Only you and I will actually know. And the guy at Gem-X. And, of course, Townsend. And one other."

"Let me guess," Burns broke in. "That other person has to be Bert Edmundson. Has to be." Barlow slowly nodded, indicating Burns was correct. "But Gem-X's not really interested in the election, are they?" Again, Barlow nodded. "Unless I miss my guess, what really interests that person at Gem-x is the Harmon lawsuit."

"That's right. They're very concerned about it. They want to get rid of it as quietly as possible," Barlow assured him. "This whole thing makes me nervous, Carter. But I had to let you know what's going on."

"As well you should, Greg. Now just what does 'get rid of it' actually mean? I assume you mean a settlement of some sort. What did Townsend say? Any real details?"

"You're right about that. They see this products liability thing as having potential to harm them far beyond the lawsuit. They want it out of the way. 'Buried,' I believe, was Townsend's word. And they don't want their parent, Standard Appliance, to know anything about it either. Some heads would roll for sure."

"One more time. What's Townsend's proposal?" At that point Burns turned off the television. He wanted to listen even more carefully than the first time. Barlow repeated his earlier statements. "Townsend's friend will provide us, the campaign, with seventy-five thousand dollars in television advertising costs. He'll work it into Gem-X's regular advertising budget with Edmundson and no one will be the wiser. That way, Gem-X's insurance carrier will not be involved in some huge settlement figure, and neither will a lot of other people at Gem-X. A reasonable settlement will get little attention."

Both men sat in silence for a moment as Burns absorbed the significance of what he had been told. Barlow broke the silence. "I told Townsend I would think about it and get back to him by the end of the week, if possible. I never mentioned your name, actually. He didn't either."

"Oh, I'm sure he didn't. Not necessary. He knew you understood I would have to get involved eventually. No real surprise there, now is there?" Burns acknowledged. He expressed no emotion. "Let me think about this. Don't call Townsend until we've talked again. Next couple of days. Maybe sooner." Burns stood up and grabbed his briefcase and headed for the door. Barlow followed and promised to wait for his call. "You did the right thing, Greg. Handled a tricky situation very well. Just let me think about it."

With that they went their separate ways, each aware of the significance of the conversation and the wildly serious repercussions if not handled carefully. That would be Burns's responsibility. Barlow was relieved to be rid of the problem Townsend had presented, at least for the moment.

During the drive home to Legend Hall, Burns resolved that no one else in the campaign would know about the Townsend conversation with Greg Barlow. Not even Kent Reed. Hiding the campaign "contribution" would be no problem, if everyone did what he was supposed to do. He was confident Bert Edmundson was a pro at juggling advertising account funds. But Caroline Harmon was another matter altogether. Getting her to settle the suit would not be simple. He determined he would have to act quickly, before his client was too emotionally involved with the suit, as he knew would be a danger the longer it went on. Refusing Townsend's offer was never even a consideration for Burns.

Florence Burns was in the kitchen preparing dinner when her husband walked in. Her back was to him when she asked, "Is that you, Carter?" without ever turning around. She was putting the final touches on one of his favorites, Marbella chicken.

"No, madam, it's Paul Newman, and I've come to take you away from all this squalor," he replied, crossing the room to the sitting area near the fireplace.

"Well, Paul, dear, you'll just have to wait until my husband and I have dinner," she teased, relieved to see him in a good mood.

He walked up behind her and gave her a quick kiss on the back of her neck. "Have I got time for one drink?" he asked, already heading for the liquor cabinet.

"Make it a short one. I'll take one, too," she said. "Let's sit in the study while the chicken cooks. It'll take just a few more minutes. Then everything's ready."

She joined him in the study and thanked him when he handed her her drink. "At least someone's in a good mood this evening," she remarked as she sat down across from him. "Perhaps I should have spent the afternoon with you rather than with Ellen Collins."

"What were you doing over there? I thought we agreed you would stay away from Ellen, especially if it was causing you a problem," he reminded her.

"Oh, I know. And I actually didn't mean to stay as long as I did. We just had a little sherry while we were going over the plans for the bridge tournament at the club next month. I thought it would take her mind off Caroline and all that. For a while at least."

"When is the tournament?" he asked.

"It's supposed to be in the middle of next month, but we won't be able to have it if Ellen doesn't get more involved. I suppose she could resign as chairman, but that would only depress her more. She asked me about Caroline's lawsuit. But I told her I didn't know what was happening right now, and that seemed to satisfy her."

"Does Ellen know I'm doing everything I can?" he asked defensively. "Lawsuits take time. We've barely begun this thing. Did she indicate Caroline was getting impatient or anything?"

"No, I'm sure she's not," his wife assured him. "Carter, you know how much Wink and Ellen appreciate what you've done for them. And now for Caroline. They feel so helpless where she's concerned because they can't do more themselves. You know how it is with them since Wink lost his business. Frankly, I don't see how they've maintained things as well as they have."

"They'll make it, Florence. And so will Caroline. It all just takes time."

"I know . . ." she began.

He saw an opportunity to help relieve his wife's anxiety about the Collinses and hopefully to help himself at the same time. "I'll call Caroline after dinner and see how's she's doing. She may have some questions and is probably too nice to bother me at the office."

CUNNING Treatment

"Maybe that would help, dear. Oh, I'm sure it would," she said, as the oven timer for the rolls chimed. "Let's go eat and then you can call her right after we finish."

※ ※ ※

His wife was still in the kitchen loading the dishwasher when Burns dialed Caroline Harmon's number. "Caroline, this is Carter Burns. I hope I didn't disturb you."

"No, Mr. Burns, Kate and I eat early. Excuse me while I turn down the television. Kate keeps it so loud," she responded. She quickly checked on her daughter who had fallen asleep on the sofa. "I'm back," she announced.

"This won't take long," he began. "I just wanted to see how things are going with you. Greg Barlow was asking about you today. So I thought I'd check for myself."

"Greg's helping in the Reed campaign, isn't he?" she asked. "I saw his wife at Kroger yesterday afternoon. She said he was excited about working with you."

"Yes, he's treasurer this time and doing a fine job. Quite a sound businessman, as well as attorney. But I'm calling to tell you that I heard from your insurance carrier yesterday about Ken's policies. No real developments, but they did assure me they're proceeding on things."

"Well, that's good to know. But I wish all this wouldn't take so long."

"Is anyone giving you a hard time about anything?" he asked.

"No, not at all, at least for now. It's just that I'm so nervous about the whole thing. It's all so complicated," she explained.

He saw the open door and stepped in. "Caroline, it's probably a little premature, but if Gem-X's lawyer broaches the subject of a settlement, I want your permission to see what exactly they might be thinking about. It never hurts to listen." He had planted the thought of settlement in her mind and waited for her reaction.

"Anything you can do will be appreciated, Mr. Burns. You know that," she said gratefully. "The case is in your hands. You just tell me what to do."

"It probably won't happen any time soon. But you never can tell about these things," Burns told her. "It might be a case they want to get out of the way." When Caroline said she heard her daughter calling, he told her to go on and he would be back to her later. "I promise to call if I see any movement on their part," he assured her and hung up.

CHAPTER 21

When Hank Ralston entered Casey's and gave his raincoat to the hat check girl, Chuck Townsend was on the telephone in the lobby and motioned for the hostess to show Ralston to his table. After about five minutes Townsend returned to the table where he found his guest well into a double vodka and tonic with lime.

"That was Ed Byas at the newspaper. He was telling me Harris has called a press conference for Tuesday to announce some important endorsements in the governor's race," Townsend informed him. "How's your drink? Ready for another one?" he asked, motioning for a waiter.

Townsend continued to talk after placing their drink order. "And while that's no surprise to most people, what is noteworthy is the announcement includes Dave Wentworth. He's Henry Long's right hand man." Henry Long was owner of the evening newspaper in Raleigh and had close labor ties. "And," he added, "if Wentworth is endorsing Harris, you can bet Long's paper will be causing Reed even more problems all the way to November. Very interesting," he remarked almost as if to himself.

As usual Ralston wanted to get to the real subject of his interest and offered no response to Townsend's political news. When the lobbyist finally paused to savor his drink, Ralston jumped in. "Have you heard from Reed's people? From the attorney in the lawsuit?"

Townsend knew it was unfair to Ralston to delay any longer, although he still found discussing the subject of the lawsuit to be troublesome. "Yes, and it looks like they're going to play ball after all. After next Tuesday and the Harris announcement, if it's what I expect it to be, they ought to be even more interested than ever. Henry Long can raise a ton of money for Harris, almost as much as Bryce Talmadge will raise for Reed. And Reed's camp knows that all too well."

"Just how interested are they in what you proposed?" Ralston persisted.

"I offered them the seventy-five thousand dollars in television ad costs, just as you said. They know the situation and what's expected in return. Meaning that lawsuit. And they know how the money's to be handled by the Edmundson Agency. Don't worry. I suspect Burns has been in tight spots like this before. You don't get where he is without pulling a few tricks. He understands what has to be done. That guy's a pro," Townsend said, trying to reassure Ralston, who still wore a skeptical expression.

"What do I have to do now?" Ralston asked.

"The next thing you do is contact your attorney handling the Harmon case. It'll be your job to convince him Gem-X wants to settle the case and how soon. You can come up with the fucking reason," Townsend instructed him.

"I can do that easily enough. Then what?"

"If it's like any other case, your lawyer will call Burns and make an offer to settle on behalf of Gem-X. You can expect Burns to haggle for a while, but not too long. Don't be discouraged by that. Remember, the campaign clock is ticking every minute. He won't take long. Believe me. He'll settle, but he has to make it appear to be a strong bargaining effort. Meanwhile you just sit back and wait to approve the final figure, then tell your carrier it's over and how well you did."

"When do I tell Edmundson to start billing Gem-X for Reed's television spots?" Ralston wanted to know.

"Not until the settlement papers are final, old buddy. When your attorney tells you they've been signed and filed in the court clerk's office, then and only then do you go to the advertising agency."

"I'll call Harry Mills tomorrow morning and get things started," Ralston responded dutifully. "What do I owe you,

Chuck, other than what I've already paid you?" he asked, aware there would certainly be something else Townsend would expect.

"I don't know just as yet. It won't be much, Hank. I might want to take a female friend on one of Gem-X's European incentive trips for your distributors like I did a couple of years ago. Something like that. I'll let you know in plenty of time," Townsend replied.

"I'm sure you will, Chuck," Ralston laughed. "I'm sure you will."

After Townsend left Casey's for another appointment, Ralston stayed for one more drink. He wanted to ponder the call to Harry Mills regarding the settlement. Meanwhile, as Chuck Townsend drove his Olds out of the parking lot at Casey's, he was also thinking about a telephone call. One he would make the next day to Greg Barlow.

* * *

"Caroline Harmon is on line one," Mary Cole announced. Burns quickly took the call.

"Mr. Burns, this is Caroline Harmon," she began. "Mother said you had called over there looking for me. I didn't get the message until late last night, so I decided to call first thing this morning," she explained. "I hope I haven't bothered you too early."

"No, not at all, Caroline. Florence and I were out last evening, so it's just as well you waited. I had called Wink about something and asked if you might be there when I couldn't get you at home yesterday. I didn't leave a message on your machine," Burns said. "I was calling to find out when you could come down to my office, hopefully this week. We need to discuss a few things, and I thought it would be easier here."

"Has there been a development in the case?" she inquired. "Or with the insurance?"

"Yes and no, Caroline. But I prefer to discuss these things with you in person if at all possible. We would have fewer interruptions here. I'm sure you'll understand," he replied.

CHAPTER 22

Caroline Harmon arrived at the offices of Burns and Walters shortly after four o'clock as arranged. She observed the activity level was what she would have expected for much earlier in the day. Young lawyers, obvious from their attire, and secretaries, equally obvious from the expressions in their overworked eyes, scurried from office to office, hellbent on something. She wasn't sure what. She only had to wait a very few minutes before being shown into Carter Burns's private office on the eighteenth floor.

"Would you like coffee or a soft drink?" Mary Cole offered as she opened her boss's door.

"Or a martini?" Burns said, as he rose from his desk chair to greet his client. "Mary must have been a bartender in a previous life. She can make gin practically sing." His secretary waited at the door for a response.

"No, nothing for me. But thank you. I had a late lunch at Mother's. Eadie, our maid, is keeping Kate for me, so I had to go by there before coming here. And Eadie never lets you leave without eating at least something. My regular sitter has exams tomorrow, so I had to fall back on good old Eadie once again."

"Will there be anything else, Mr. Burns?" Ms. Cole inquired in her customary professional tone.

"No, thank you, Mary. Please hold my calls," he replied, as his secretary closed the door behind her.

Burns sat down opposite his client in the sitting area away from his massive desk. He had a small fire in the fireplace, as he often did on certain occasions, keeping the thermostat set low enough for just that reason. Some psychiatrists he had heard of used tropical fish to help a patient relax. Burns preferred scented logs. "How are things at home these days? And little Kate?" he asked warmly.

"Well, keeping up with her is a full-time job in itself. She's quite a handful, and the house is really too big for the two of us now. I've thought about an apartment or small condominium. But I'll have to wait until this suit is settled to see exactly what I should do. Or even could do. I'm not sure what I can afford," she responded.

"I'm sure Kate misses her father," Burns stated affectionately.

"Actually, no. Sometimes she asks about him. But during his residency, Ken was away from home and at the hospital so much of the time, she wasn't used to having him at home. That may change later when she sees other kids with their fathers. You know how that is."

"Maybe by that time she'll have a father figure at home, Caroline. You're quite an attractive woman. Remarriage should be a definite possibility, if you don't mind me saying so," Burns remarked.

"Of course not. Thank you. But my hands are full now with Kate, the house, and my part-time job. Not to mention the lawsuit. I've got to get my own life straight first, before I take on anything else, particularly dating, much less a husband," she said candidly.

"I can certainly appreciate that," he agreed. Before she could speak further, he took the opportunity to get to what he had wanted to discuss. "You mentioned the lawsuit. And that's what I need to discuss with you. We've had an offer from the defendants. I warned you this might happen. They—"

"A settlement offer," she interrupted him.

"Yes, but first I want to give you the background, so you'll understand what they're thinking, where they're coming from."

"I'm sorry. Please go ahead," she said, once again leaning back in her chair.

"Don't apologize, Caroline. I understand your anxiety. You have every right to be concerned. But maybe I can answer all your questions with an explanation of everything involved, as least as I see it," he said and began in a very deliberate, very relaxed tone to explain the basic terms of the law of products liability, particularly how it related to a manufacturer such as Gem-X. As he went through the litany, she nodded that she understood or at least indicated she was following him to a degree.

Finally, she had to seek the answer to the only question she cared about. "How much are they willing to pay to settle?" she bluntly broke in at the first opportunity to interrupt without being rude.

Without hesitating, Burns responded. "They've offered three hundred and seventy-five thousand dollars."

As he carefully placed another log on the fire without turning to face her, he said, "I don't know about you, but I think I'll have Mary make me one of her special martinis before she gets away for the day. It's about time for her to leave," he remarked. "She gets here so early, and some of the others definitely lack her magic with gin. I know I do."

"Sure. If that's an offer, I'll join you," Caroline accepted. She was certain she needed a boost after contemplating what she had just learned.

When they were both holding brimming glasses, Caroline reminded Burns of something he had said earlier. "When this all began, you said the measure of damages was Ken's earning power over his lifetime. Don't you think three hundred and seventy-five thousand dollars is way off the mark more than just a little bit?" She elaborated, "Ken was a gifted plastic surgeon. He wasn't paid minimum wage. They have to be aware of that."

She was right, and that was the really tricky question Burns knew he could not avoid. If he could get her past that one point, he was confident about the rest. He saw his only hope was to appeal to her special needs and circumstances.

"Caroline, Ken was a fine surgeon. Gifted, no doubt, in so many ways. No one can argue that. But you have to look at the other factors a judge and a jury will have to weigh heavily in this type of case. Particularly in the circumstances of Ken's death." Burns then went into considerable detail about the difficulty of proving what actually caused her husband's death. He methodically recounted the facts of the case, subtly taking the position of devil's advocate. The matter of the missing ground wire warning had never been mentioned by Burns, although his expert had noted it in a report the attorney had not shared with his client.

"The bottom line," he said, "is that we actually do not know beyond a reasonable doubt what happened, what caused Ken's death." At that point the issue of Gem-X's failure to put the warning sign on the dryers had not come up. Discovery had only begun. No depositions of the manufacturer been taken. No experts had officially been brought in. "The coroner said it was 'heart failure *possibly* attributable to electrocution'." Burns accentuated the word "possibly." He continued with his carefully thought out presentation. "But there's another factor that will definitely attract the defense. You know how Ken wasn't exactly Mr. Fix-it around the house, despite his efforts. That will come out in court, first in your next deposition. They will jump on that like a duck on a June bug. Rest assured." He paused and poured himself another drink from the batch Mary had prepared.

"And Gem-X markets a pretty good product line. Standard Appliance, their parent company, is one of the best, most respected in the country. Half, if not more, of the members of the jury will own one or more of their products and probably be darned pleased with them. They don't turn out garbage. And they'll have paid experts to testify to that. And there were other appliances in your basement near Ken. Each one will have to be ruled out. Who knows for certain what Ken actually touched last? There was even the old clothes dryer which, I believe, you said Ken disconnected himself. And that's my point. Gem-X is going to want to find out every little detail, some of which may not be in our favor. And all of that discovery takes time, lots of it. Conservatively speaking, and I know what I'm talking about, this suit could easily go on for two years before even getting before a jury." He paused and then played his best card. "Caroline, I have to ask. Can you afford to wait that long in your financial situation?" There it was. Out on the table with all the simple logic that he could apply. He rested his case while all he had said sank in.

When she didn't respond immediately, he went further. "I agree that Ken's earning power was much higher than the settlement offer. That could be proven with no difficulty at all. But to even get to that point, that dollar figure, the damages, we have to first prove what caused his death. That's the whole problem, and so long as any doubt may remain in the minds of the jurors, you will be running a big risk, a major risk. That's basically the decision you have to make, Caroline. If you're a gambler, we'll proceed. It has to be your decision. I can only advise you, help you make an informed decision, whatever it may be. And I want you to think about it. Think long and hard," he lied. "I know it won't be easy, but only you can make it."

They talked a little longer before she told him she had to go and fetch her daughter. After she left, he wasn't sure she had been convinced and was fairly certain she wasn't at that point. It would take more persuading from him, perhaps. She said she would call if she had any more questions, leaving the door open for him to make the pitch one more time.

But he had gone too far to back off. It was all out there, or so he thought, for her to consider. Burns knew he would have to wait and see what course she would choose. He wished that somehow there was a way he do more to help her with her decision, but he was unsure there was any way he could at that moment. He recalled his favorite thought from Ayn Rand to the effect that "somehow" always means "somebody." But who? he wondered.

※ ※ ※

All the way across Raleigh, Caroline Harmon's mind raced from one situation to another as she drove. Everything Carter

Burns had told her since even before the lawsuit had been filed, all the advice, all the caution, the thoughtful encouragement from someone she had known since early childhood, it all was so important. Then there were the details, the facts about Ken's death, what they knew and all that they did not know. The mountainous task her attorney had outlined of proving how Ken had died and what the jury might or might not believe. Finally, there was the money factor, which meant so much to her future and her daughter's. As she drove, she never turned on the car radio, craving silence to help her put everything in a hopefully sane perspective.

She slipped into the kitchen of her parents' home through the back door and hugged her daughter, who instantly ran to clutch her mother around the knees. Kate and Eadie had been mixing up chocolate chip cookie batter, the child's favorite. Kate still had the gooey spoon in one hand.

"Eadie, I need to talk to Mother and Daddy for a few minutes. If you'll stay past your bus time and watch Kate for me, I'll make my standard offer to drive you straight home. I promise," she almost pleaded. Eadie gladly agreed to stay, allowing Caroline to join her parents who, Eadie told her, were in the study.

The stereo was playing softly as she entered the room. She was correct in thinking her parents had been sitting there for some time saying very little to each other. Then seeing her father standing at the wet bar, she said, "Okay, Dad, twist my arm. I'll join you in whatever you're having, but not as strong, I assure you. On second thought, make mine a Scotch on ice, unless you're out," she said, certain that no Scotch was not even a remote possibility.

"Hello, darling," her mother said from her chair as she set aside the *Town and Country* she had been thumbing through. "Please, Wink, do as she asks. Caroline, here, sit by me," she said and motioned toward the overstuffed chair next to the sofa.

"Thanks, Mother. I believe I will. Looks right tempting. I'm bushed," she said, moving the needlepoint pillow to one side and gladly accepting the drink and cocktail napkin from her father.

"Can you stay for dinner?" Ellen asked. "Eadie fed Kate some time ago. But your father and I were waiting."

"We'll see how Kate holds up out in the kitchen. But first I want to ask your opinion about something. It's pretty crucial right now," their daughter began. "I just came from Carter Burns's office. He spent over an hour explaining a lot of things to me. A lot of important things, and I need to think through them with someone."

Wink and Ellen sat listening to their daughter without interrupting. She repeated a great deal of what her attorney had told her. Particularly about the law and the problem of having to prove exactly what caused her husband's death. As best she could, she explained how products liability laws in North Carolina were so much in favor of the manufacturer, due to the influence of the tobacco industry. "What it all boils down to," she concluded, "is that Gem-X, the company which made the dryer, has offered three hundred and seventy-five thousand dollars to settle the case." With that she took a long swallow of her Scotch.

As he made his way back to the wet bar for more bourbon and shaved ice, Wink Collins was the first to speak. "Hell, Ken would have made more than twice that a year, two years from now. As soon as he quit being an indentured servant to those cheap, no-talent bastards he was working for. When I think about how those two . . ."

"Yes, Dad, I know. We've been through that one often enough, even when Ken was alive. But that's over for all of us. Now what we have to consider—and please help me—is whether I should settle or go on and run the clear risk with the suit. Mr. Burns will do whatever I say," she assured them.

"What did Carter say about going on with it?" her mother inquired.

"He said, if I understand it all, that the case could go on for some time, even years. I'm sure he's right. Dad, correct me if I'm wrong, but it took over two years just to settle your business accounts when they bought you out. And I don't have the means to carry on that long without help." As soon as she said that, she wished she could retract every word. But it was too late.

"Caroline, you know how much we're sick, that we can't..." Ellen began and reached to touch her daughter's arm.

"For Christ's sake, Ellen. Don't get off on that again," her husband demanded. "Can I turn off that damn music?"

"Wink, please, don't shout. I don't think my nerves can take it if you do," his wife pleaded in a remote, exhausted voice.

"Oh, how I damn well know you can't. You can't take anything," he snapped. "The only thing you can take is more booze and lately you don't take that too damn well."

Their daughter broke in. "Look. Thanks a lot. But no thanks," she said rising from her chair. "If you two can't stop thinking about yourselves for just one lousy minute, just one goddamned stinking minute, then I have to go." On her feet, she added, "I need some advice. I need it badly, but I sure came to the wrong place for that. You'd think, after all these years, I would at least have learned that simple fact, now wouldn't you?"

"Wink, please, make her stay," Ellen pleaded as she watched her daughter storm toward the door. "Please say you're sorry, Wink. Go ahead. Tell her you're sorry, Wink. You're the one who shouted."

Reaching for Caroline's half-empty glass, he said, "Let me freshen this, Caroline. Sit down. I'll be quiet. But I *am* going to shut off that noise." He silenced the stereo.

"I want to check on Kate. I'll be right back," she said. "I promised Eadie I'd take her home, so I need to speak with her first." When she returned to the study, her mother was no longer in the room. "Where did Mother go," she asked.

"She went upstairs. Don't worry. She's all right," her father answered and handed her a fresh drink.

"Oh, I'm sure of that. The great escape artist from all responsibility herself. Old 'Exit Ellen.' That's what Jenny Burns and I used to call her when we were growing up. She gets better at it all the time."

After she went back to where she had been sitting, Caroline decided to try one last time and asked, "Dad, I want to take that settlement offer. But I don't want to be a fool. Ken made more than that. Kate has a lot of growing up ahead of us both. And that's going to be expensive. You know I don't want to be a burden—"

"Caroline, you're never a burden. You never have been," her father interrupted.

Looking at him, she wanted to take back the entire moment. She realized his eyes had tears in them as he stared blankly at the bookcase full of family photographs.

After a moment, he spoke. "I should have known years ago not to trust those bastards." He was back in his own sad reverie, his own problems. "They planned the whole thing, and I helped them by trusting them. All along they played me for a damned fool. And I must have been just that. They were nothing. Nothing. But old Wink Collins made them something, and then they turned on me like cur dogs."

She saw it was useless in continuing. Caroline wanted to take back the entire moment. She realized she should never have asked, should never had brought her problems home to her parents. Gently, she sat her drink on the coaster on the table. She leaned over, kissed her father's forehead, and left the room to retrieve her daughter, to retrieve her own sanity for the decision she had to make.

The next day Caroline called Carter Burns and told him she had thought through the settlement offer and all the rest he had said. Quickly, she authorized her attorney to accept the offer and draw up the necessary papers. The sooner the better, she had said. He asked what had made her decide. But she merely said she had slept on it and knew it was the right thing to do. She said, "It all boils down to a matter of trust, and you know I have to trust my own instincts and, of course, you, Mr. Burns."

CHAPTER 23

The Senate of the United States had frequently been characterized as the "world's most exclusive club" and understandably so. Two people from each state are elevated to positions of power that even they often, at least initially, have trouble comprehending. Of course, it rarely takes very long for a senator to slip comfortably into the mantle of power and prestige, and to wear it well, some better than others. One of the most successful of the membership in achieving and wielding power was the late senior senator from North Carolina, The Honorable Evan Potter Hayden.

In many ways Evan Hayden was an enigma in his home state and eventually so across the entire country where he twice campaigned unsuccessfully for the presidency. Hayden had few, if any, close friends. Instead he had a small army of devoted admirers and supporters who took pride in understanding that no one of them was any closer to the great man than they were. From the time he was first elected to congress in the late 1930s and right on through his years of public acclaim as a senator, Evan Hayden maintained a strong, persistent hold on his constituents. He championed their causes, and some said he fought crusades for what he believed was right.

In his senate committee chairmanships, he bravely tackled organized crime and took on the powerful insurance industry, when both appeared untouchable and definitely avoidable to his fellow members. Senator Hayden combined a folksy, somewhat reserved demeanor with a brilliant intellect and an unforgettable smile to become the first of many who later realized the immense force and value of television. In the 1950s Senator Hayden's televised duels with bosses of organized crime and the greedy CEOs of major insurance companies appearing before his committee won the hearts of many Americans, many of whom had been put to sleep by President Eisenhower and insulted by the whining theatrics of Vice President Nixon. Evan Hayden's dogged questioning of individuals many saw as villains, particularly the pin-striped, arrogant insurance giants, made him a hero whose strength of character was unavoidable. His resonating "Do you understand the question?" became a household phrase.

Although Evan Hayden didn't succeed in being elected president himself, he was imminently successful in getting other things he wanted. Frequently, they had red hair and wore his favorite Arpage. Happily married to a red-haired beauty since he was twenty-five, Hayden remained married until his death, but never was he loyal. He had a penchant for women, especially red heads or an occasional strawberry blonde. That was a well kept secret among his senate staff who worked hard to keep it a true secret in Washington and, of course, at home in North Carolina.

Among the senator's staff not long after World War II was a recently graduated attorney from the Tar Heel State. His name was Carter Burns, and he became fascinated with the rumors about his boss's secret passions. Just out of Duke University Law School, and new to the nation's capital, Burns saw getting ahead quickly as a priority. In his mind information was a formidable means to do just that. Later that inclination would prove invaluable.

* * *

Another arrival in Washington from the same state was the freshman Congressman Jonathan Fowler in 1944. The thirty-one-year-old Fowler brought with him his prematurely white hair, a quick wit, and a bag of promises to keep back home. Fresh from a desk job in Seattle during the war, Jonathan Fowler was ready to do his fighting as he best knew how—with his elegant tongue and a secret weapon, his stunning wife Lenore, whose Camay face framed by strawberry blonde tresses she kept in a slightly loose bun, made her quite a contrast to most of the other not so blessed congressional wives.

Lenore Fowler was ahead of her time in ambition as well as looks. Unwilling from the beginning of their marriage to be the silent partner keeping the kids and homeplace tidy, Lenore engineered the plans and called the shots in her husband's political career. Their daughter, Anne, was age four when the family arrived in Washington and an exact replica of her mother head to toe. The three Fowlers looked almost regal in the family photograph on each year's Christmas greeting to their constituents. But over time constituents noticed that suddenly *all* they saw of the Fowlers was on Christmas cards. For long stretches of time, the Fowlers stayed away from North Carolina, and many voters at home became disenchanted.

It only took a short while before the Fowlers' annual holiday message began to fail to ignite the proverbial home fires for the absent congressman. Rumblings were soon heard from one end of Jonathan's district to the other. While some wanted him kicked out of office, others just wanted an answer to why he had forgotten where home actually was. When the rumors eventually reached Lenore Fowler's ears, she quickly called several of their closest political confidants who confirmed what she had first heard from a Raleigh newspaper reporter visiting the capital.

She and the reporter were having lunch at the Willard Hotel when he gave her the first word of any trouble back home. "Lenore, I'm not saying Jonathan has anything great to worry about," Jim Scott was saying, "at least right now. But you have to understand that, if he continues to spend so damn much time in Washington like he has for four years, he might find the discontent at home more than he would care to deal with in the next election. It's happened before," he warned her, "and it would be a damn shame to add Jonathan to that casualty list."

Lenore listened closely to everything her friend said. She was about to ask another question about the district, when Senator Evan Hayden entered the coffee shop accompanied by someone Lenore had never seen before. Hayden immediately walked over to Lenore's table with the young man in tow. "Well, Jim," the senator began, "doing a story on Jonathan Fowler's most delightful contribution to Washington, I see." Everyone laughed and Lenore pretended to shoo Hayden away from the table. "Oh, by the way, Lenore, Jim I want you to meet another fine product of the Duke law school. This is Carter Burns. He's working in my office now. Concentrating on the Lend Lease thing."

"I'm pleased to meet you, Carter. But I really must get back to the office, Senator," Lenore said as she slid out of the booth. "Jim, why don't you do a real story on the senator. The folks back home never tire of hearing about the great things he accomplishes up here." With that bit of flattery, Lenore shook hands with Evan Hayden, then Carter Burns and left the hotel. She had absorbed everything Jim Scott had told her. Indeed, Lenore Fowler left the hotel on a definite mission.

Lenore's first step was to meet with the members of her husband's Washington staff. Subsequent telephone calls back home led to a secret summit scheduled in Raleigh with Jonathan's key supporters. That session was held in the Hunt Room at the Brookside Country Club only days later and lasted well past midnight. The Hunt Room was presided over by the large oil portrait of the late State Senator Casey who would have enjoyed such a gathering. However, Jonathan was not able to attend due to an important vote on the floor of the House that evening. Lenore had called the meeting and everyone knew it was hers to begin with. No questions asked.

But were such meetings, such contacts, *all* that was needed, she asked herself on the flight back to Washington. The election in 1950 was only a year away. She felt she had to have a powerful ally to help carry the district again and in a big way. Still a closely guarded secret, Jonathan was planning to run for the United States senate in 1952, and that required a big win for him in 1950.

It was rumored that junior U.S. Senator Neal Hardison was going to retire for health reasons. If Jonathan was to make a move, it would have to be then. As her flight landed at National Airport, she glanced over and fixed on the Senate Office Building. At that moment she acknowledged there could be no more powerful friend to have on her side than Evan Hayden.

It was only a matter of ten days after her return to Washington that Lenore was able to make her own move to secure the future. She, too, had heard about Evan Hayden's favorite weakness and was certain she fit his criteria. To make sure, she wore her shoulder-length strawberry blonde hair down and softly curled when she and Jonathan attended a cocktail party in honor of actor Jimmy Stewart. The next day President Truman was presenting a special metal to Stewart for his work on behalf of refugee children in Europe. Lenore made certain Evan Hayden was to be there. She also resolved that the Hollywood star's hand would not be the warmest hand the senator would shake that night.

CHAPTER 24

The winter weather in Washington, D.C. changed almost as often as some politicians changed their minds on any given issue. And January 21, 1947, was no exception. What began as a mild, mostly sunny day gave way initially to slow, gray rainfall, then to driving snow. By early evening, a three-inch layer placed a hush on the normally busy city with an additional two to four inches predicted by the next morning, a Saturday, when the coal smoke from the city's forest of chimneys would render the pristine covering a dull grayish smudge.

Carter Burns was working at his desk in the Senate Office Building since early that morning. Having graduated with honors from the law school at Duke University, Burns applied for and landed a clerking job on the staff of Senator Evan Hayden, the very powerful senior senator from Burns's home state of North Carolina. The eager, aggressive young attorney quickly parlayed his excellent writing skills to obtain the pick of the office assignments. His current project, along with Lend Lease, had particular significance to his boss. By the first of February, which was only a few days away, Senator Hayden wanted to announce his long-awaited position on crucial welfare legislation which was pending in the Senate, and, if the senator's instincts were correct, the legislation would prove to be a pivotal issue in the elections of 1948, both nationally and at home.

However, it was a Friday and, as a quick glance at the snow out his curtainless window assured him, Burns decided the project would wait. It was nearly 8:00 P.M. and traffic in the nation's capital was practically nonexistent. Most government

CUNNING Treatment

offices had closed early, due to the dramatic weather developments, and only the foolhardy or dedicated remained on duty.

Burns had only his old, brown overcoat and a flimsy black umbrella he found in an office closet to protect him, as he began the walk of several blocks from the office to his one room apartment in the Georgetown section of the city.

Nearing the Willard Hotel, where a long line of black taxi cabs waited to carry prominent hotel guests to fashionable parties for the powerful, who never let an unexpected snowfall interfere, Burns noticed Senator Hayden's personal car parked near a little-used side entrance to the famous landmark hotel. From the white exhaust bellowing from the rear of the shiny, black Buick, Burns realized the car was running and could see the driver sitting patiently on the front seat. Burns crossed the street to be opposite the hotel and the senator's car. Deciding to wait and see what was transpiring, he took a post beside a large oak tree and slightly tilted the umbrella to partially cover his face.

Even though it seemed longer due to the cold which stabbed at his wet feet, it was only a few minutes before the famous senator emerged from the Willard's side door and quickly ushered his companion into the back seat of the cozy, warm car. Due to his close proximity to the merry scene and the hush produced by the blanket of snow, Burns could hear both persons laughing, and he easily recognized the senator's beautiful friend, none other than Lenore Fowler, the stunning wife of North Carolina's second term congressman, Jonathan Fowler, whose future Burns had heard to be threatened at home because of his emerging liberal viewpoint and his all too frequent votes to prove it.

Certain aspects of Senator Hayden's private life had long since gone beyond the scuttlebutt stage and had become closely guarded secrets. But Burns had learned the senator had two compelling passions in his life: expensive, single malt Scotch and beautiful redheads. Lenore Fowler's striking face with bright green eyes and the hint of a dimple was surrounded by a cumulus cloud of softly curled strawberry blonde hair—close enough for

Hayden's preference. However, happily married with a teenage daughter, the senator was careful never to be too open with his affairs, never wanting to embarrass his loyal wife.

Acting on impulse after Senator Hayden's car slowly drove off into the increasingly heavy snow, Burns crossed the street and entered the Willard through the main entrance. The dark, muffled hush of the outside contrasted strongly with the hotel lobby's bright lights and the loud chatter of dozens of people milling between the marble columns and the feathery green palms in the cavernous room. The crowd in the hotel's popular bar had spilled out into the lobby, where many in the well-dressed guests clutched highballs, as if bracing themselves for whatever the night would bring—weather or otherwise.

Hoping to take advantage of the confusion created by the noisy mob in the lobby, the young attorney assumed his most innocent expression and authoritative voice when he told the desk clerk what he needed, indeed, what he had to accomplish. "My name is Carter Burns," he began, when he finally had the desk clerk's attention. He realized using his real name was a risk, but if asked to prove his identity to the clerk, it was one he had to take.

"I work in Senator Evan Hayden's office," he continued, staring directly at the clerk, "and he asked me to retrieve some papers from his suite. The senator was here earlier and forgot to take the papers with him when he left. They're important, and he needs them badly tonight." He knew that if the clerk called the office no one was there, nor, he correctly supposed, was anyone in the senator's suite.

The clerk's expression didn't change. Burns persisted on his mission, although still unsure just what he was doing. "If you could give me a key to the suite, I'll get the papers and bring the key right back to you." At the moment he concluded his plea, a particularly boisterous foursome from the lobby crowd verbally attacked the desk clerk on two fronts, so the clerk decided to solve the easy problem first. He handed the key to the suite to Burns and returned to confront the two impatient couples who were shouting in order to be heard over the increasing noise in the lobby.

For years Senator Hayden maintained a suite at the Willard Hotel. For the record, he kept it for business meetings and the occasional use of important constituents from North Carolina who might be visiting the nation's capital. However, it was common knowledge among the senator's office staff that the politician himself used the luxurious suite for his own more personal purposes on a regular basis. The hotel had standing orders to keep the bar in the suite well stocked with the powerful man's favorite Scotch, and there were always to be fresh flowers on the table in front on the fireplace, which the female guests never failed to appreciate. The flowers in a Waterford vase were always to be roses and always red.

"Thanks," Burns said, quickly accepting the key from the harried clerk. "I'll be right back," he promised, heading toward the elevators, still unsure about what he was doing.

* * *

With the key to the suite in one hand and the battered umbrella in the other, Carter Burns walked directly to the elevator which opened just as he got to it. He quickly entered the walnut paneled cubicle, looked at the key for the room number, and punched the button for the eighth floor.

When he arrived on the eighth floor, Burns followed the corridor around to suite 801. Across from the door to the suite was the service elevator. Smiling, he acknowledged Senator Hayden's appreciation for logistics. Use of the service elevator enabled the senator to avoid the hotel lobby, and the elevator would deposit the noted statesman near the secluded side entrance where Burns had seen the senator's Buick waiting.

Burns listened momentarily at the door to determine whether anyone else might be in the suite. Finally, confident his boss and Lenore Fowler had been alone, as he had expected, Burns entered the suite and immediately closed the door behind him. The lights in the parlor were still blazing, and there were two empty whiskey glasses beside the red rose on the table in front of the fireplace. There was still a remnant of a flame.

The door to the bedroom was ajar. He slowly entered the room. Only one bedside lamp was lighted. The bed was obviously the scene of recent use, and there was one towel on the floor beside the bed. On the other side of the bed, he found a small, black leather book which was peering from under the bed's dust ruffle. The cover of the book had the initials "LPF" in one corner in gold. Inside he found the addresses and telephone numbers of the "who's who" in North Carolina politics and not just a few impressive Washington entries. Not actually expecting to find Lenore Fowler's monogrammed panties at the scene, the scheming young lawyer found something even more valuable. He carefully slipped Lenore's little black book into his suit pocket and quickly left the suite as he found it.

Returning to the hotel lobby, Burns tossed the key back to the desk clerk. He acknowledged his reentry into the cold January night was somehow better than when he had earlier left the Senate Office Building. His adrenaline had given him newfound warmth as protection against the night, and, perhaps, whatever the future might hold.

CHAPTER 25

"Carter, I must apologize again for having to cancel on you the other day." The soft, yet firm southern voice belonged to Lenore Fowler. "But when I woke up that morning, it was all I could do to even breathe. It's my allergies. They're the worst I can ever remember. Didn't have one problem when I was in Alaska on that trip, not one. I went with Jonathan and saw my own doctor that day. Now I have two different inhalers and two pills I have to take twice a day. If this doesn't work, I don't know what I'm going to do."

"Lenore, I more than understand. My wife suffers year round. If it isn't ragweed, it's mold or whatever's flying through the air that day." Burns wanted to sound sympathetic, but hoped his caller was wanting to talk about more than just allergies.

"I'm calling to set another time. The rest of today is free for me, and tomorrow is open as well," she offered. "I'll accommodate you however I can, after standing you up like that."

Quickly glancing at his calendar for that day, Burns saw only two appointments for that afternoon and knew his secretary could use her considerable charm and ask his clients to reschedule with him. After all, he thought, they need me more than I need them. And he was determined to meet with Lenore as soon as possible. Important campaign developments were happening almost daily, and he had to get to her before she made a move which couldn't be undone. "You can't put the toothpaste back in the tube," he was fond of saying.

"How does one o'clock today sound?" he asked.

"That's perfect. Perfect. Jonathan's speaking at the Rotary Club luncheon and may not be here. If he got paid for those speeches, it would suit me much better. But I had a feeling you wanted to see me alone anyway," she replied. Lenore never missed anything.

"I'll be there at one," Burns declared, preferring not to respond to her observation about being alone. After she reminded him about the tricky turn off Highway 19, one most people missed the first time they drove past it, the conversation ended with pleasantries neither was sure about.

As he drove toward the Fowler farm thirty miles south of Raleigh, Burns reflected back over the previous two weeks following Reed's formal announcement. Things had been happening much faster than even he had imagined they would. People were taking sides quickly. There had been a veritable avalanche of endorsements, some expected, some coming as complete surprises to both camps. He knew if wily State Senator Will Hardy had *not* endorsed Stewart Harris, then that would have been a surprise. Reed's endorsement by the North Carolina Industry and Trade Association was also no surprise to anyone. But when the state's Farm Bureau took a "wait and see" position, well, that was totally unexpected and interpreted as favorable for Reed, at least at that moment. Now, if I can only isolate the Fowler machine, Burns thought as he drove, that will amount to a certifiable coup. And he was confident he had the means to accomplish that very thing.

Next he reviewed his conversation with Greg Barlow about finances. The previous evening Barlow had assured him the money was coming in. Mostly from expected sources, and smaller amounts from generally all across the state. Neither Barlow nor Burns discerned a pattern from where the money was coming from. But it was a little too early for that, Burns understood. Thinking about money reminded him of the Harmon lawsuit settlement, which had been signed two days earlier. No, he said to himself, I'm not going to spend any more time thinking about that. To Burns the Harmon matter was ancient history, and he buried it in the darkest recesses of his mind. He had other things to concentrate on, none more important than Lenore Fowler.

The mistress of Woodlawn, as the Fowler farm was known, greeted him at the door herself. "Gracious, Lenore, Ponce de Leon would be proud. You do look marvelous. 'You look marvelous'," he repeated in a weak imitation of Billy Crystal.

The older yet still beautiful woman enjoyed the flattery and gave her caller a quick kiss on the cheek. "Carter, you better just save that talk for someone much younger," she laughingly admonished him. "Come on in. We'll have something in the library. How about tea or some fresh lemonade? We didn't grow the lemons, but I did squeeze them. Jonathan loves lemonade. Insists I keep a cold pitcher in the refrigerator at *all* times." As she led the way down the hall, Burns couldn't help but admire the way she carried herself and the dynamic presence she had always exhibited wherever she was.

Finally, seated in front of a sunny bay window, Lenore spoke first. "Carter, it looks like your pal Kent Reed intends to run a campaign we can all be proud of." She was acknowledging the professionalism and high road Reed had taken, starting with his announcement. She was also aware of the all-powerful role Burns was playing in the campaign.

"You know, Lenore, that's exactly what's intended," he replied, realizing that it was his turn to be flattered. "We fully intend to see that it stays that way, at least from our side. We can't do much with the rest."

"I'm sure you will. I can't imagine anything to keep this from being a clean race. But one thing's for certain. It's going to be a watershed election for North Carolina. A lot of hard issues have to be faced head on. Some things like education and taxes can't be dodged any longer. Not if North Carolina's economy is going to stay competitive," she asserted.

"I couldn't agree with you more, Lenore. The state's going to suffer if any mudslinging starts. The Democratic Party has to come out of the primary united, or we'll just flat out hand the election to the ultra right-wingers the Wooten supporters represent. We've been down that road before and got stuck in a dead end."

"I know. How well I remember. No, we can't let that happen," she agreed, but then went right to the matter at hand—whatever it was Burns had on his mind. "Now, tell me, Carter, what's the reason for this visit? You must know I always want what's best for North Carolina. What else is on your mind today?"

"Truthfully, I'm asking you for a negative. I won't go so far as to ask you to endorse Reed, but I am asking that you *not* endorse Stewart Harris." There. He had said it and let it sink in.

Her response was not long in coming. "Carter, we've worked with the Harris people for a long, long time, a very long time. You know that as well as I do, or you wouldn't be sitting here."

"Of course, Lenore. I'm well aware of your alliances in the past. They're more than clear. I'm just asking the Fowlers to stay on the sidelines this once."

Seeing she was debating her reply, Burns deflected her thoughts by inquiring about the health of her son, Kip. "That plane crash scared the hell out of a lot of people. How's Kip doing now?"

"Very well. He's complained about all that physical therapy for his leg, but who wouldn't? But Kip's as strong as an ox. Much like his father. Luckily, he doesn't even have my allergies."

"In my opinion, Lenore, Kip shouldn't risk being on the wrong side in this campaign. He's looking much further ahead and doesn't need to make a tactical error at this juncture. One that might reflect on his judgment in some minds."

"Carter, at my age I don't need a lesson in politics from you or anyone else," she bluntly assured him." She seemed to resent the turn of the conversation to her son or at least be uncomfortable with it. Burns was not sure which. "And I'm not so certain Harris won't be elected. What makes you so sure right now? It's early yet."

"Oh, I'm sure all right. Times have changed in this state. Reed will catch on. But I'm not willing to take chances." With that remark Burns reached into his coat pocket and took out a small black book and gently placed it in her lap.

She stared at the small volume for several minutes without speaking. Then she picked it up, opened it to confirm what she thought, and closed it again. "How long have you had this?" she finally asked. Her words were soft, yet firm. Her green eyes left what was in her hand and fixed on her guest.

"I've had what you're holding for a long, long time. I found it in Senator Hayden's suite at the Willard Hotel."

"And I suppose you were pretty proud of yourself for that. You always were proud of yourself for just about everything, as I recall."

"I do the best I can."

"For yourself," she shot back. "I feel certain you don't give a damn about anyone else, or you wouldn't be here now doing this. And what were you doing in Evan's suite anyway? Were you invited? I never knew him to entertain office staff there."

"That makes no difference, Lenore. But certain people would find the story I can tell very interesting."

"No doubt they would." She paused and again looked straight into Carter Burns's eyes. "You're a real piece of shit, you know that? Pure glorified shit. You know what you can do with your damned story."

"Yes, that I do, and so do you. But I won't go away. I'm here to make a trade, Lenore."

"You mean blackmail, don't you?" she insisted. When that remark failed to draw a response, she continued. "All right, Carter. Tell me. What do you *really* want out of this? I can't wait to hear. You wouldn't just waltz in here without wanting something for your valuable time. Now would you?"

"Just what I've already told you. It's that simple. I want you to keep your people neutral in the primary race. That's all. Stay away from anything to do with Harris or anyone associated with that bunch. You do that, and your secret will remain just that, a secret."

"Kent Reed's election is pretty important to you. Before now, I had no idea how much. That's for damn sure. You'd obviously stop at nothing to get what you want." Throwing the black book back into his lap, she snapped, "Here. Take your precious little bombshell. You've held onto it for all these many years. So just hold onto it as long as you want." That surprised him, but he accepted it willingly.

Lenore leaned back, suddenly appearing slightly weary. "Kip's future is too valuable to risk. He doesn't need to take sides in other races," she said, adopting Burns's logic. "You've got my word on the governor's race. Won't be too hard to sit though this one. Stewart is no real prize anyway." She paused, then went further. "I could stand the embarrassment. But it would only hurt Kip and probably kill Jonathan."

"You mean Jonathan doesn't know? Kip looks nothing like him—or you for that matter. He's a dead ringer for Evan Hayden."

"Those who at least suspected the truth when they looked at Kip are all dead now. And Jonathan's too decent a man to ever question anything like that. He worshipped Kip from day one. No, he never asked me or even made a remark. Jonathan desperately wanted to believe Kip was his son. That's all there was to it in his mind. But the resemblance, I have to admit, between Evan and Kip is striking." She paused staring out the window, back into the distant past. "Evan would be so pleased with the way Kip has turned out. He would love to know Kip actually might make it where Evan always wanted to be."

Sensing she was calmer and perhaps even relieved, finally being able to discuss Kip with someone, Burns asked, "Has Kip ever said anything about not looking like either of his parents?"

"That's enough, Carter. Enough." Tears were in her eyes. In a low, faraway voice, she told him, "Now get out."

"Lenore—"

Raising her voice and choking back her tears, she said, "I said get out! Now. And I hope to hell you get what you truly deserve, Carter Burns. Eventually you'll outsmart yourself. Ambitious creeps like you usually do. God only knows what drives you. But you're going to drive yourself right into a brick wall some day. I only hope I'm there to *read* about the wreck," she snarled. "Now kindly get the hell out of my life."

Burns knew there was nothing more he had to say to Lenore Fowler. During the drive back to Raleigh, he congratulated himself on a victory only two people would ever know about. And that suited him well enough.

CHAPTER 26

At first Burns refused to even discuss Chuck Townsend's suggestion that the two of them meet. When Greg Barlow told him Townsend's message, Burns emphatically instructed Barlow to inform Townsend there was "no earthly purpose for any meeting. Period." He angrily slammed the telephone receiver in Barlow's ear, furious that Townsend had the nerve to think they had anything to talk about. He considered their business finished, over with weeks ago.

However, he was mistaken. Within an hour Barlow was again calling him. "Carter, Townsend won't take no for an answer." Barlow realized Burns had been angered by the first call and had dreaded making the second one.

Burns simply exploded this time. "Look, Greg," he practically shouted into the receiver. "I appreciate the fact that you're only relaying messages. But you tell that lowlife son of a bitch our business is finished. Settled. And while you're at it, remind him that I could cost him a few clients during the next session of the legislature if he doesn't keep his smelly ass out of my way. A couple of phone calls and he'll be lucky to have street people for clients. Chuck Townsend and I have nothing to talk about, not one damn thing. He should know that and, if he doesn't, you damn well better make sure he does."

It was abundantly clear to Barlow how serious Burns was on the subject of Chuck Townsend. He was also aware that Burns did not make idle threats. When Burns went after someone, it was an unholy war. Nevertheless, Barlow had additional instructions from Townsend. Closing his eyes as if to avoid a collision, he decided to blurt out the rest of what Townsend wanted him to relate to Burns. "Carter, Townsend said you should either pick him up in your car on the corner of Melrose Place and Lake Avenue tomorrow at two o'clock, or he could meet you at the Hyatt Hotel on Hilton Head Island this weekend. He said you would know what he meant."

Barlow thought those two alternatives were slightly strange, but they were not strange to the man who heard them. Burns slowly sat back in his chair. He realized there was definitely more to Townsend's request than he first thought. Much more. And he had no choice but to agree. Not wanting to alert Barlow to any significance in Townsend's message, Burns acquiesced. He admitted, "It might not do any harm to see what was on the bastard's mind. Tell him I'll pick him up tomorrow. Tell him he's to be alone and to get right to the point. Whatever he has to say, I want to hear it quick."

* * *

What started as an early autumn season suddenly began to look like an early winter for Raleigh. All the folk weather "experts" throughout North Carolina pointed with pride to all the signs so eagerly noted during the summer just ended. A bumper crop of spiders whose webs were thicker and stronger than any in memory. Frantic activity by the squirrel population gathering nuts. And the abundance of black woolly worms with a single orange spot on their backs. Forecasters noted that all the signs were there. But Carter Burns only saw the cooler weather as indicative of one fact—the election was getting closer and closer. Reed's primary victory over Stewart Harris had proven to be even easier than Burns had predicted. But the general election was proving to be no cakewalk. Conservatives were lashing out at Reed from all angles.

"And the last thing I need to do is fuck around with Chuck Townsend," he muttered to himself as he drove toward the designated rendezvous. When he arrived at the corner of Melrose

Place and Lake Avenue, he was grateful to see that Townsend had at least chosen a part of Raleigh where neither would be recognized. Burns was right on time, and Townsend was waiting. Townsend stooped over and looked inside, making sure Burns was driving.

Sliding into the passenger seat of the Lincoln, Townsend was conscious of the fact that he and Burns had never had a conversation before, at least that he could remember. Despite their having been at numerous Bar and political functions and legislative sessions as lobbyists, he did not recall any words having been exchanged between the two, pleasant or otherwise. Barlow's instructions to "get right to the point" were still on his mind, so within seconds he began his business.

"I'm sorry I had to get your attention the way I did," Townsend said, in his mind meaning the reference to Hilton Head, but hoping to get off to a civil start with the man who had yet to look at him.

"All right, Chuck. I'm here just as you asked. Now tell me real quick what it is we have to talk about," Burns said, still without looking toward his passenger and pleased about the green traffic light but little else.

"Carter, your visits to Hilton Head weren't as business-oriented as you might want people to think. Nor as secret."

"What's your point? What does Hilton Head or anything else for that matter have to do with you and me or anything else I might give a damn about?" Burns demanded.

"There's not a lot of time for games, my friend. You know that," Townsend told him, but wanted to underscore his point. "I saw you and Marge Preston there more than once. The last time was when I was on a boat pulling into Harbour Towne. It was the night before Marge was killed, if I remember correctly. Before that I—"

"Look, Chuck, I get your message. Okay? Now suppose you tell me what the hell you're after," Burns interrupted angrily.

Townsend, however, was not to be intimidated or talked down to. "Don't get your back up, counselor. You've got your price.

We've already been there once, you'll no doubt remember," he said, obviously referring to the Harmon case.

"That's settled, Townsend," Burns reminded him. "What else is there?"

"Settled only partially, *Burns*." Townsend was determined to match him tit for tat. "Look. You're not in a court room. Get off your fucking pedestal and listen. Reed's goddamned election means quite a bit to you. That's no fucking secret, now is it? But for just a second let's focus on what it might mean to someone else for a change. Namely me."

"I'm listening."

"I want two things from you. Two."

"And they are?"

"I want your fee in the Harmon case. The one the insurance carrier paid."

For the first time Burns glanced at Townsend. He was incredulous. "You want the damn fee?"

"The way I see it, it's my fee. I earned it when I put that deal together. You'll get plenty more once Reed's elected. You know that."

"You said two things," Burns reminded him, wanting to end the conversation as soon as possible.

"The next one might surprise you. But I'm dead serious about it," Townsend informed him.

What Burns heard next almost made him pull over to the curb and kick Townsend out of the car. But Burns had to acknowledge he had little choice but go along with Townsend. The fee he could book as payment for legal services to another attorney. No problem. Townsend's second demand, however, would be trickier and harder to live with.

CHAPTER 27

The brisk November breeze blew the leaves across the driveway as Carter Burns walked to pick up the Sunday morning newspaper. Placing the paper in its plastic wrapper under his arm, he pulled his red plaid robe tighter and yawned. He was still tired from being out until the early morning hours attending another party for governor-elect Kent Reed and his wife, the soon-to-be first lady, Charlotte.

The election two weeks earlier had been alarmingly close and bitterly contested. Reed's campaign had managed to maintain a high level of decency and decorum, despite being savagely mauled by his opponent, strident conservative Tom Wooten, on more than one occasion. Stewart Harris's endorsement after the primary battle had been helpful in the rural western part of the state, and even Harris's Aunt Louise had managed to find a few nice things to say about Reed. The Democratic Party had held together after all. Toward the last of the general election race, the Fowler camp issued a thoughtful plea for party unity without ever mentioning Kent Reed by name. But any call for unity had been appreciated and the omission overlooked by many and particularly understood by Carter Burns.

Back in the house, Burns was followed to the study by Amberjack, their golden retriever, who immediately curled up in front of the fire. Sitting down in front of the oversized glass coffee table, Burns opened the newspaper and spread it out on the table.

He had left a large cup of coffee waiting on the table and took a long sip. Methodically turning the pages, he found what he was after. On page four the latest of Reed's appointees were pictured.

The story capped a three-column photograph of a smiling governor-elect accompanied by Carter Burns, "prominent Raleigh attorney," who Reed had said he would nominate as the next Attorney General of North Carolina, as soon as he was sworn in and the legislature convened. With any governor's nod, an attorney general's election by the legislature was historically a foregone conclusion. Burns' selection would be no different. Next to Burns stood an obviously elated "Charles Townsend, well known lobbyist." At the urging of Burns, Reed had named Townsend to his staff in the important capacity of Chief Legislative Counselor. The newspaper article further described Townsend as a "spy who had come in from the cold," Townsend's former role having been one of opponent of many governors' legislative proposals. Burns thought of Townsend somewhat differently and in less favorable terms. "That son of a bitch," he muttered to himself, but loud enough to cause Amberjack to look up at him quizzically.

In the statement announcing his latest appointments, Reed again thanked the people of North Carolina for their vote of confidence. "Confidence in me, the goals I have addressed, and in the people around me who will help improve the quality of life for all who live in and even visit our great state." The latter was a subtle acknowledgment of the money the Reed campaign had received from outside North Carolina. That allusion to "visitors" had been Burns's idea. He looked at the newspaper picture as would a coach of a well played, hard fought game won by an obedient quarterback and many others who had adhered well to the "playbook," as he termed his campaign instruction manual. Details. Details. Details. All in the hands of one Carter Burns. Next he flipped rapidly to the sports section to read about the results of Duke's latest gridiron adventure the day before against Virginia. He took delight in finding another victory for a Burns team.

Across town in a more modest section of Raleigh, Caroline Harmon carefully eased open the front door of her small condominium, so as not to awaken her daughter. The condominium in Heatherwood was small and more economical than the house on Valley Brook she sold right after settling her lawsuit. The brightly decorated two bedroom, two bath unit provided her a place to regroup, and more importantly, cut expenses. Returning to her kitchen with the newspaper, she poured a cup of Instant Maxwell House and sat down at the oval walnut kitchen table she had found at a yard sale and painstakingly refinished. Ken would have been proud of me for that, she admitted to herself.

Caroline glanced only briefly at the lengthy obituary and photograph of Judge James Foster, who had approved the agreed upon settlement of *Harmon vs. Gem-X* months before. Next she turned to the society section where the lead story was the latest of many Kent Reed victory celebrations the previous evening at Brookside Country Club. The party was given for the governor-elect and "his charming wife" by Ellen and Wink Collins and Florence and Carter Burns. Caroline did not have to be told that her attorney had probably insisted on the Collinses being given credit for the event while Burns had paid for everything. The newspaper photograph of the party attendees was in color, but in being reproduced turned everyone's eyes red. "I bet Mother's were red long before she got there," Caroline uttered softly, still hoping Kate would remain asleep a little longer. The article was one of those in which everyone had a cutesy nickname. It seemed to Caroline that, although she had grown up in the city, she only lately had realized that Raleigh society relished members called things like "Pudge," "Tut," "Gabby," "Kiki," "Cootie," "Mimsy" or worst. She giggled out loud and wondered if in reality those were their *real* names and the obligatory quotations were the only affectations.

Abruptly, her treasured solitude was broken by "Mommy, I'm hungry." Caroline instantly gathered her daughter into her lap and pulled her close as she helped the child with her twisted bath robe. "Look, Kate," she said, pointing to the picture of her parents. "There's Grandma and Grandpop."

"I want to see," the child demanded.

"They're right there. See?"

"They look pretty," Kate observed and smiled at her mother.

Caroline refrained from saying what flashed across her mind. "Yes, they do, sweetie."

Also in an accompanying photograph were Bob Henry and his wife along with Bryce T. Talmadge, whose left arm was tightly clutching the shoulders of Greg Barlow. It was one of those occasions each of "Bryce's boys" had come to expect, knowing their mentor would never miss an opportunity to have a touchy-feely moment.

In the business section of the newspaper, Caroline was drawn to a small story about a shake-up in the home office of Gem-X Corporation, Inc. The article described the overriding financial pressures being experienced by Gem-X and attributed them to the economic slump affecting the nation as a whole. "Americans have fewer dollars to spend on white goods, and that directly impacts on Gem-X's sales," the writer clarified.

The article went on to state that Robert Phillips, president of Gem-X, had taken early retirement but would be staying on in a consulting capacity for one year. Sweeping personnel changes at the company were detailed, including cutbacks reflected upon by "long-time vice president Carl Bateman" as "part of the hard choices Gem-X has to make to survive in this economy," Bateman was quoted. Henry "Hank" Ralston was noted as having been promoted to vice president of marketing, but a newspaper typesetting error gave that portion of the article a unique twist when a filler became part of the story.

"Gem-X has grown and matured, all the while exhibiting the flexibility and willingness to make the hard decisions which will ensure its future survival and leadership in the industry. Ralston's promotion is one of those decisions," the article said, citing statistics released to support Ralston's credentials. "Clothes do not make the man," was the next line.

In the section of the paper devoted to political events, Caroline came across a photograph of Senator Kip Fowler. The accompanying story said the "dynamic, young political star" had been in Raleigh meeting with Democratic Party leaders from around the nation at their request. They made no secret their mission was to get Kip Fowler to agree to run on the party's ticket as vice president. The conventional wisdom was that Walter Edwards, popular two-term governor of Indiana and immediate past chairman of the National Governors Conference, would win the nomination for president. His only opposition was a one-issue quack congressman from Louisiana who had little appeal outside Bourbon Street. Walter Edwards was clean-cut to a fault, progressive, and had a smile women lined up for. A ticket led by Edwards, at age sixty-one, required a younger running mate to attract first-time voters, as well as those with first-time mortgages. When Harold Williston, a three-term congressman from Massachusetts withdrew from consideration—"My young family and I will be honored to continue to serve the people of Massachusetts"—anyone with sharp political instincts turned to Jonathan "Kip" Fowler, the aggressive, moderate junior senator from the Tar Heel State and Lenore's son.

Patient long enough, Kate decided she wanted to turn the pages all by herself. But when she saw the photograph of Kip Fowler, she stopped suddenly. "Mommy, he's a nice man," the child commented.

"That's Kip Fowler, Kate. He's from North Carolina. But he works in Washington, D.C. He's a real important person," Caroline explained.

Lately, the child had become conscious that her friends had fathers and she did not. "Does he have a daddy?" she asked.

"Yes, he does, Kate. But he's not in the picture," was her mother's observation.

Carter Burns well understood that and so much more.

FINIS